Grant Me My Name

To Gabriella

Loyalty binds us!

Alex
x

Best wishes,

Grant Me the Carving of My Name

An anthology of short fiction inspired by
King Richard III

With a foreword by
Philippa Gregory

Edited by
Alex Marchant

Sold in support of Scoliosis Association UK

SCOLIOSIS
ASSOCIATION (UK)

First published 2018 by Marchant Ventures

Copyright © 2018 the contributors

Editorial selection and introduction copyright © 2018 Alex Marchant

Further copies can be ordered from Alex at AlexMarchant84@gmail.com

The right of the contributors to be identified as the authors of this work has been asserted in accordance with the Copyright, Design and Patents Act, 1988.

All rights reserved. No part of this publications may be reproduced, stored in or introduced to a retrieval system, or transmitted, in any form or by any means, electronic, mechanical, photocopying, recording or otherwise, without the prior permission of the copyright holder.

ISBN: 9781730715693

Cover illustration: © 2018 Riikka Katajisto

To

Dr John Ashdown-Hill

For his tireless dedication to scholarship and the
Ricardian cause

Contents

Foreword by *Philippa Gregory* — ix
Acknowledgements — xi
Introduction — 13
Purgatory *Marla Skidmore* — 17
Long Live the King *Narrelle M. Harris* — 26
Five White Stones *J. P. Reedman* — 30
Dames Joanne's Talke Thinge
   Larner and Lamb — 45
Bowyer Tower *Wendy Johnson* — 51
Ave Atque Vale *Frances Quinn* — 55
Buckingham's End *Richard Unwin* — 60
Abduction *Joanne R. Larner* — 78
The Beast of Middleham Moor *Alex Marchant* — 85
Joanna Dreams *Máire Martello* — 110
14th April 1471 – Blooding *Matthew Lewis* — 115
Easter 1483 *Alex Marchant* — 129
Myth and Man *Narrelle M. Harris* — 131
Kindred Spirits: Return of the King
   Jennifer C. Wilson — 140
Beyond the Rood *Wendy Johnson* — 155

Foreword

Philippa Gregory

This collection has come about – as so many good things do – from a dream and a joke. Authors Alex Marchant and Wendy Johnson exchanged short stories about Richard III and joked that they should make a collection of stories about England's most controversial king. Editor Alex Marchant spoke to other authors and the dream of a book of short fiction looking at aspects of Richard – real and imagined – turned into reality: this book, published in support of Scoliosis Association UK (SAUK).

Richard's history has been obscured by Tudor propaganda, by no less an author than William Shakespeare, and by the mysteries that still surround this king. With the charm of the Plantagenet family and all of their determined ambition, the youngest son to Richard of York was never going live an ordinary life.

He was a boy when his father made his first attempt on the throne of England and he grew up as his older brother's most trusted commander. But with the energy that helped him overcome the physical difficulties of serving as a knight in armour with scoliosis of the spine, the religious conviction that guided him, the passion that led him to his first runaway marriage and the intense desire to succeed, Richard led an extraordinary life.

Even his death was exceptional – and misremembered. He was the last English king to lead a cavalry charge in battle, and the last to die in battle. He died defending his throne, as a crowned king of England against a rival who was – at the time – a usurper without royal rights. His death is woefully recorded: the Shakespeare play has Richard calling for a horse to ride into his last charge: '*A horse! A horse! My kingdom for a horse!*', so often quoted as a coward calling for the means to escape. In fact, his last words were '*Treason! Treason! Treason!*', as he went down under the blows of former friends and allies.

It's a more dramatic end; it's a more tragic end. Can there be any doubt that Shakespeare did not use it because it casts such doubt on the claimant to the throne and his supporters – Shakespeare's new patrons, the Tudors?

Richard's burial and the subsequent rediscovery of the lost grave is another unexpected event in his story. At last this most troubled king can rest in peace, and this anthology is one of the many tributes that have been paid to him.

Yorkshire
October 2018

Acknowledgements

We would like to thank all the contributors for generously donating their work to this anthology, including Poet Laureate Carol Ann Duffy for allowing us to use a line from her poem 'Richard' for our title, Riikka Katajisto for her fantastic image of King Richard, Dan Rendell for designing the cover around it, and of course Philippa Gregory for kindly providing a Foreword.

Some of the pieces have been previously published in some form and we would like to acknowledge permission to reproduce them here.

'Purgatory' was originally published as Chapter 6 of *Renaissance: The Fall and Rise of a King* by Marla Skidmore.

'Long Live the King' was originally published in *Scar Tissues and Other Stories* by Narrelle M. Harris.

'Bowyer Tower' and 'Beyond the Rood' were originally published in *The Court Journal: The Magazine of the Scottish Branch of the Richard III Society*.

'Buckingham's End' was originally published in *A Wilderness of Sea* by Richard Unwin.

'14th April 1481 – Blooding' was originally published as Chapter 2 of *Loyalty* by Matthew Lewis.

'Easter 1483' was originally published in *The Order of the White Boar* by Alex Marchant.

About the illustrator

Riikka Katajisto knew quite early what she wanted to be when she grew up, having felt a strong desire to express herself in an artistic way as soon as she learned how to walk. She went straight to Kokkola's Nordicartschool after high school to learn different art techniques and then to Kankaanpää Artschool to perfect her artistic and creative expression, there developing her own inimitable style.

From childhood Riikka has been inspired by history, particularly the mysterious twilight wanderings of medieval times, and King Richard III especially has been an inexhaustible theme – sometimes with an artist's freedom to stretch the truth of events in his life. Her art is aimed at history lovers who don't take things too seriously – she often tosses humour into her pictures to make them laugh. She has published two children's books, *Plantagenet* and *Herman the Dreammosum*, and made many short films using a variety of movie-making tools.

Website: https://riikkanikko.blogspot.com/
Blurb: http://www.blurb.com/books/4496331-plantagenet
http://www.blurb.com/books/3582284-herman-the-dreammosum

Introduction

In early 2016 I had a dream – quite literally. One of those between-sleep-and-waking dreams. A vivid image. Of a frightened boy caught in a snowstorm, with a strong hand outstretched, reaching towards him. I recognized it was on a moor, had a powerful feeling that moor was up above Wensleydale, just a few miles from where I live. And I thought I knew who that strong hand belonged to.

The imagination is a funny thing. I got up, showered, had breakfast, walked the dog – went about my daily routine. And within a couple of hours a story which became 'The Beast of Middleham Moor' was almost complete in my head. And of course I was right about whose hand it was.

At risk of spoilers, I'll not name the person. But suffice to say, he was a major character in the two books for children I'd recently finished writing – and I think I 'missed' him.

As an author, when one has spent, perhaps, two or three years in the company of certain characters – whether fictional, or real, historical and dramatized – I suspect it's not unusual to miss them once you've finished telling their story. In my case I missed some so much I've started writing a third book of tales of their lives. Some, of course, will not reappear for various reasons, which may not be within an author's control if they were real people, with real lives, and real outcomes – not always good outcomes. Perhaps that sense of missing – or even 'loss' – was what prompted my fragmentary dream.

I'm not alone in feeling drawn to my own characters – and this book is a testament to that. A single character this time, one a dozen authors (as well as the distinguished writer of our Foreword) have been moved to give life to in various ways. A historical character, of course. And so a real living person at his own point in time. And one who holds a fascination for many people – a fascination that seems strange to some others, although perhaps less so since the momentous rediscovery of his centuries-lost grave in 2012. And I'm not the only person – fiction writer or otherwise – who has had similar experiences leading to a creative impulse.

And here are some of the fruits of those impulses – a collection of short stories inspired by that man. In my case I soon knew the main protagonist of my story – the boy, lost – would have scoliosis, and once the story was completed, I knew it could be a potential fundraiser for the worthy cause of the Scoliosis Association UK (SAUK), which helps support people with the condition and their families. This is a charity that no doubt would have been close to the heart of the man who prompted all these stories, whose own scoliosis only became widely known following the excavation of his grave.

This man was, of course, maligned in the decades after his death by writers living under the king who stole his throne: a little over a century later his good reputation – which led the city council of York to call him 'the most famous prince of blessed memory – was in tatters thanks to a damning depiction by perhaps the world's greatest playwright – writing his plays for the granddaughter of that same king. This anthology is one of many works that seek to bring the real man back into focus – the man about whom the Scottish ambassador of the time said, 'nature never enclosed within a smaller frame so great a mind or such remarkable powers'.

I'm delighted that one of the Looking for Richard Project team responsible for finding his grave, Wendy Johnson, herself also a writer of fiction in addition to her historical research, has contributed two pieces to this anthology and been instrumental in persuading me to bring all these stories together. Perhaps it's unsurprising that, having worked so closely on such a project, she has been inspired to write about the man concerned.

Other moments of inspiration involved a bouquet of white roses seen at the foot of a statue, a chance remark about bringing a medieval man to the present day, and the real-life dream of a young woman who lived five centuries ago and gave her heart to a man she never met. Perhaps you yourself have had similar moments. If so, maybe you would like the chance to share them. At the end of the book is a call for contributions to a possible future anthology. In the meantime, I hope that you enjoy this one!

This book is dedicated to one of the inspirational people whose painstaking work over a number of years led to the finding of the grave that ultimately prompted this book: Dr John Ashdown-Hill, who sadly died earlier this year – a great loss to scholarship, especially of the late fifteenth century, and of King Richard III in particular.

Alex Marchant
October 2018

Purgatory

Marla Skidmore

An adapted excerpt from *Renaissance: Fall and Rise of a King*

After his death in battle on Redemore Plain, King Richard III discovers his soul must, like every other, be guided through the spiritual trials of Purgatory by a celestial mentor. Yet when they reach Eden, the last stage before the ascent to heaven, Richard's spiritual guide, Franciscan monk Father Gilbert, finds his young charge strangely reluctant to take the final step ...

Richard's hand hovered over the bishop.
'Should I move him?' he mused aloud.
Seeing his friend's gaze swing towards his queen, the monk smirked inwardly, knowing exactly what he would do. Richard was quite unaware of his obsession with the queen. Whenever they played chess he would advance her and then manoeuvre her all around the chessboard, instead of utilizing his pawns, knights and rooks. He watched Richard slide her forward and with humorous exasperation reflected that, despite spending countless hours attempting to teach him the finer points of the game, Richard continued to be a truly terrible chess player. Instead of using that cool assessing brain to strategize, he allowed emotion to rule his moves.
This approach was totally out of character for the man the monk had come to know so well – the scholarly thinker and leader of men, who had been England's last warrior king. Having been Richard's guide and counsellor whilst he worked through his penance to satisfy the justice of heaven for his transgressions, Father Gilbert felt he had come to understand him well, but there were facets of his character that still remained an enigma. Richard's journey

to redemption had long been completed. Yet he was reluctant to take the final step into the next world. Something held him back. It was time to get to the bottom of his determination to stay here. The Guardians were becoming impatient.

'My friend, for my own selfish reasons I would delay your departure for as long as possible and will be deeply saddened when you leave, but you must see that you cannot remain here indefinitely.'

Richard raised his head and looked inquiringly at the monk, a hint of amusement lurking behind his deep-set blue eyes.

'Why ever not? I am comfortable here ... I lack nothing.' He let his gaze range around the vast library that they were sitting in. 'These shelves contain a copy of every book and manuscript ever written.' I have been humbled and honoured to have been allowed to debate with and listen to the thoughts of some of humanity's greatest and most wise souls ...' He couldn't suppress a chuckle. 'And been amused by the cogitations of the most foolish ... Rest assured, monk, I am content,' he murmured and, with a half-smile, slid his knight into Father Gilbert's trap.

The monk huffed in silent irritation, but didn't immediately pounce. It would be more instructive if Richard had time to perceive his error before he made his move. Father Gilbert sometimes wondered whether his protégé deliberately played badly just to bait him. Nevertheless, he was determined that Richard should become at least competent at chess before their ways finally parted.

'Be that as it may, but your period of atonement was completed countless decades of mortal time ago,' he pointed out dryly. 'No other soul has lingered so long here in heaven's ante-room ...'

And there it was, that flicker of resistance behind Richard's eyes.

The monk decided to confront head on his

charge's disinclination to leave Purgatory.

'You have been tested, undergone correction and cleansed your soul of every residue of sin. Why are you so reluctant to embrace your heavenly destiny?' he demanded.

Pushing up from the deep leather armchair in which he sat, Richard strolled down the length of the book-lined room towards the tall mullioned windows that dominated one end. His lean figure was delineated by bright spring sunlight as he stood motionless, gazing reflectively out over the lush fertile valley that spread out below him. A tiny movement in the muscles at the corner of his mouth was the only outward sign of the troubled thoughts that plagued him. Sighing, he turned towards his mentor with a quizzical look.

'And what exactly is my heavenly destiny, Gilbert? What will I experience for all eternity when I leave Eden?'

The monk moved a pawn and looked up with a benign smile.

'Why, Richard ... you already know what is waiting for you ... absolute peace ... perfect happiness.'

Hearing the confidence in the monk's words, Richard briefly closed his eyes.

Peace ... happiness ... for him ... how could that be...?

He swung round and slowly retraced his steps down the length of the room. Lowering himself back into his chair, he studied the state of play on the chessboard; his knight was doomed and he suspected that his bishop would go next. With a mental shrug he accepted the loss of his knight and sent his queen to waylay the monk's bishop. Having made his move, he sat deep in thought for long moments, then clearing his throat, he turned determinedly towards the man with whom he had developed a bond closer than friendship, closer than family.

'You told me long ago, that once it had been made ready, each soul would know when the time was right for it to ascend into the Afterlife.'

Alerted by the edgy tension in Richard's voice, Father Gilbert abandoned the game. Reclining against the worn leather back of his chair, he folded powerful arms across his deep chest. Stretching out his legs, he crossed one ankle over the other and raised his sharp eyes to Richard's face.

'Tell me what is troubling you, Dickon,' he commanded. 'What weighs so heavily on your soul that you will not allow yourself to find the heavenly repose you laboured so long and hard to achieve?'

Richard flinched at the monk's use of that almost forgotten diminutive of his name; he struggled to push away the vivid recollections of his past life that it conjured up in his mind. Resting his elbows on his knees, he bowed his head. His eyes absently traced the grain of the ancient wooden floor beneath his feet whilst he tried to marshal his thoughts and find the words to explain himself. Finally, drawing in a deep breath, he spoke in a bleak voice.

'That's just the point, Gilbert ... I do not feel ready to leave here ... So much remains unresolved in my mind ... I am not fit ...' Richard's voice trailed off. He raised his eyes and the monk was taken aback by the depth of pain that he saw there.

His bushy silver brows drew together 'Sweet Jesu!' he swore silently in self-recrimination.

How had he missed this?

Feelings of compassion and guilt warred with each other inside the monk. Somehow, he had let the young king down. Father Gilbert began to question himself ... Had he become complacent because Richard had undertaken every task and trial he was set with fortitude and courage? And yet ... having mentored and guided countless transitory souls as they travelled along their personal road to redemption here in Purgatory, never once had he known one hesitate in this way, questioning the final judgement of heaven and resisting reunification with the Creator.

The monk pushed aside the low table on which the chess set lay and leant forward.

'Explain this foolishness that has taken root in that agile brain of yours,' he demanded gruffly.

Richard gave a hollow laugh, and with a grim twist to his mouth he began to speak.

'My name is synonymous with evil. In the mortal world I am the hunchback killer king. The most heinous crimes have been laid at my door.' In a flat, strained voice, he continued. 'After Tewkesbury I murdered Henry VI and his son Edward of Lancaster. I executed my brother Clarence – drowning him in a butt of Malmsey. I usurped England's throne to which I had no right. I killed my nephews. I poisoned my wife in order to incestuously marry my niece. My place in history is amongst the most reviled and evil villains that ever existed. How can someone whose reputation is so mired in infamy find peace in heaven?'

Sensing the deep anguish that lay behind them, the monk listened to Richard's words with growing concern. His state of mind was far worse than Gilbert had at first envisaged. A surge of anger flowed through him. Why had Richard not come to him with his fears and doubts instead of tormenting himself for so long?

The monk rose swiftly to his feet. Towering over Richard he began to speak, but then his mouth snapped shut to hold back a threatening stream of reproachful words. Mutely shaking his head, not trusting himself to speak, he moved across the room to stand in front of the massive stone fireplace. For long silent moments he scowled down into the leaping flames, then began to prowl back and forth, his rapid strides causing the skirt of his rough woollen robe to swing dangerously close to the burning logs.

He stopped abruptly and, in a voice, made harsh with unease and worry for his friend, he snapped, 'This …' He swallowed, then demanded sternly, 'This self-castigation must stop immediately!' From beneath brooding brows he scrutinized Richard's unhappy face. 'Think carefully before you answer, Richard. Which are you in danger of accepting? Heaven's affirmation of your soul's purity, or the vile image of you created by Henry VII's propagandists and the Tudor chroniclers who curried favour with the paranoid, murderous dynasty he founded? Which should take precedence in your mind?'

Richard drew in a shaky breath, his mouth tightening a fraction at the censure and thread of anger he heard in his mentor's voice, but he raised his chin and looked the monk straight in the eye.

'The truth of a man's reputation matters, Gilbert. In the eyes of all of humankind I am a soul beyond redemption.'

The monk snorted impatiently. 'It matters not how you are regarded in the mortal world if heaven judges you fit to enjoy eternal life with God.'

Richard's shoulders slumped in resignation. 'Cease lecturing me, Gilbert. I know you have the right of it ... but it still torments me to know that throughout all eternity, I am fated to be the monster king.'

Instinctively the monk reached a comforting hand towards him, but then he hesitated and drew back. The realization dawned on him that throughout their long association, he and Richard had concentrated so hard on working to free his soul from all taint of sin, that in the process his emotional psyche had been neglected. In this unquiet state of mind, he most certainly could not leave Eden; there would be no peace for him in heaven.

The monk found himself in a situation that he had not foreseen, that he had no real experience of dealing with. He slowly paced the length of the room, vainly searching his mind for a way forward – a way to his ease his young friend's anguish.

A heavy, drawn-out silence descended upon the room, as each man wrestled with his unhappy thoughts.

Richard shifted restlessly in his seat, his troubled gaze falling upon the abandoned chess game. He saw that he had exposed his queen, placed her in danger. Leaning forward, he picked up the tiny, intricately carved chess piece and stroked it with a tender forefinger. She reminded him of his own delicate Anne ... the dainty, playful sprite of his childhood ... who was married against her will to that arrogant pup Edward of Lancaster, when her father, the Earl of Warwick, turned traitor. Whom he'd ransacked the stews of London for, after his brother Clarence had hidden her from him – putting her to work as a scullion maid in a cook shop, so that he could keep his greedy clutches on her inheritance ... His precious love, whose frail, grief-stricken body had not the strength to fight when sickness struck after the death of their beloved son ...

A touch on his shoulder brought Richard back to the present. He looked up to find the monk gazing remorsefully down at him.

'I have let you down, Dickon,' he sighed heavily. 'I should have recognized your feeling of unworthiness and not allowed it to fester and grow as it has done. I feel somewhat at a loss – not equipped to deal with the dilemma we now find ourselves in. You are questioning divine judgement and resisting the natural progress of your soul. I must seek advice from the Guardians – in the eons of their existence they must surely have come across a situation such as this before.' He gave a rueful chuckle. 'The mentor now himself needs mentoring.'

The monk's fingers briefly tightened in a gesture of comfort, and he turned and strode across the room. But, struck by a sudden thought, he paused in the doorway.

Richard had received heaven's blessing and absolution, but this rare and complex soul had yet to forgive himself!

Resting his hand on the wide wooden frame, he turned back to look at his friend.

'To some degree we are all the masters of our own fate, Richard. Whilst I am gone, perhaps you should re-examine the events that took place during the last years of your earthly life and ask yourself why you still consider yourself not fit for heaven. Why does the Tudors' invention of the demonic King Richard hold so much power over your mind?'

Hearing these softly spoken words, Richard's eyes widened. He searched the monk's face for a hidden meaning, but could not penetrate its bland inscrutability.

Could he bear to re-live that time in his life when his whole world had turned to ashes and crumbled away, when in the space of two years he had lost everyone he most loved – his brother, his son and his wife? When, in the depths of his grief, he had underestimated, until it was too late, Margaret Stanley's dangerous obsession to place her son on the throne and his own vulnerability to the poisonous web of rumour, treachery and betrayal that she and her allies spun around him.

With a sigh Richard rested his head against the high back of his chair. As uncomfortable as it was, Gilbert's advice was sound. The Guardians would not allow him to linger in this sanctuary forever. It was time to unlock the door to his painful memories.

The soft thud of the library door as it closed behind the monk's retreating figure and the spit and crackle of apple logs burning in the hearth were the only sounds that broke the intense silence that descended upon the room.

About the author

Marla Skidmore grew up in a small medieval city in northern England where she met and married her soldier husband. She lived a typical military life in various postings around Europe and the UK before returning home to study, emerging with a dual honours degree in English and history and a Master's in literature, with which she went on to become a college lecturer.

Having dabbled in writing since university, Marla began to write seriously during a prolonged career break. Her first novel – a romantic murder mystery set during the

Napoleonic wars – was put aside when Richard III's grave was rediscovered. At lunch with university friends during the ensuing controversy about his reburial place, she speculated about what he would have made of all the fuss and was challenged to write a story: 'Do one about Richard in blue jeans.' The idea took root and the result was *Renaissance: The Fall and Rise of a King*. Her Richard is not in blue jeans, but she did bring him into the twenty-first century – in her own way. She has been diverted from her earlier novel once again: she is now writing a sequel. *Renegade* is about that most loyal of Richard's friends, Francis, Viscount Lovell.

Amazon:	mybook.to/TheRiseofaKing
Facebook:	www.facebook.com/MarlaSkidmoreAuthor/
Twitter:	www.twitter.com/marlaskidmore44
Goodreads:	www.goodreads.com/author/show/17748507.Marla_Skidmore

Long Live the King

Narrelle M. Harris

Elizabeth leaves white roses at the statue's feet. A sharp little spur of sorrow takes her every time.

Workers dug up his mortal feet, all unknowing, before anyone learned the rest of him was buried here. Distal and proximal phalanxes. Metatarsals and cuneiforms and taluses. The foot bone connected to the ankle bone, the ankle bone connected to the shin bone. The small king with the bent back connected to the hard earth.

Once, this little hole into which he'd been thrown had been the floor of a priory. Then it was car park. Elizabeth supposes it's a miracle he only lost his feet, poor Richard.

Shakespeare transmuted him into a grand old villain, charming and treacherous. These days new battle lines are drawn: good king or bad? Child-killer or slandered Christian?

Elizabeth thinks he's both; she thinks he's neither. She thinks that method, motive and opportunity were collectively very murky 530-odd years ago and a lot of questions remain unanswered.

She thinks maybe he didn't deserve to be hacked at after his death, the post-mortem blows so hard they cut grooves in his bones. Maybe he didn't deserve to be dumped with his hands still tied, his head bent up against one end of the hole, before they piled on the dirt (in his grave and on his reputation) and tiled him in. Tarmacked him in.

Elizabeth's sister Celia thinks she's foolish, with this *tendresse* Elizabeth has for a long-dead king. What does it matter if he killed his nephews or not (and he probably did)? What possible difference does it make now?

Because it's so unfair, Elizabeth wants to say.

She can't honestly say why this king's pitiable end moves her so much she brings him flowers every month. She read a story once, perhaps, where all the truths are questioned, or where all the truths were repented. A story where he was a fully textured human and not a cautionary tale about tyranny.

Richard was brave, in his time. The scoliosis that twisted his spine didn't keep him from honours on the battlefield. A good administrator, by all accounts. Perhaps he did one truly terrible thing. Perhaps he was only blamed for it. Henry had more motive, some say. *Cui bono?* Who benefits? Henry certainly would never have gained the throne had the boys lived.

Elizabeth lays the York roses at Richard III's metal feet. Behind her is the story of his life in one tourist attraction. Opposite, his bones (minus his feet) lie in the cathedral, stained glass streaming coloured light on to the limestone tomb when the time of year is right.

'In another world,' Elizabeth tells his statue, 'someone loved you for exactly who you are, and you loved them back in just the same way. In some other when and where, you're the best version of yourself. And you're happy.'

*

In some other when and where, a short man with a bent spine pauses by a statue. He's slight and his eyes are kind. A little boy grips his father's fingers with one hand. In the other is a posy of daisies.

Richard lifts his son up in his arms and holds him while the boy places the daisies at the statue's feet. They look up at her face, the sun shining behind her like a halo.

'I don't think Queen Bess killed her sister,' says the boy.

'Nor do I, Neddy,' says his father. 'Some say so, but she was so wise in other ways. Perhaps she made a terrible mistake. Perhaps she was only blamed for a terrible thing.'

Neddy climbs up and stands on the plinth by the posy.

He wraps his skinny arms around the statue's hips. He closes his eyes.

'What are you wishing?' asks Richard, smiling indulgently at his son.

'I wish for her to be happy in some world somewhere,' says Neddy. His cheek rests on the metal hip of the queen. 'Jack says it's silly, that I like Queen Bess.'

Richard leans against the long metal skirts of their favourite monarch.

'It's not silly to be kind, or to try to see both sides,' says Richard. 'It's a good-hearted thing, to want to be fair. But do you know what else is important?'

Neddy nods. 'To be your best self every day.'

'The attempt is as worthy as the achievement,' says Richard. 'And forgiveness is a kindness when we can't quite manage our best. We can always try again tomorrow. And what is our motto?'

'Loyalty binds me!' laughs the boy, and he trustingly topples from the base of the statue into his father's arms.

Neddy is almost too big for this game, but not yet. Richard catches his son and swings him around, puts him on the path again.

'Be loyal to your promise,' says Richard. 'Be your best self.'

'Every day,' agrees Neddy.

Half-way home to Anne and the girls, his sisters, Neddy wants to feel what it will be to walk like his father. He stands upon his father's feet, his upraised hands held in his father's strong grip, and Richard takes strides just long enough to make his little son feel big.

About the author

Narrelle M. Harris writes crime, horror, fantasy, romance and erotica. Her 30+ novels and short stories have been published in Australia, the USA and the UK. Award nominations include *Fly* *by Night* (nominated for a Ned Kelly Award), *Witch Honour* and *Witch Faith* (both short-listed for the George Turner Prize), and *Walking Shadows* (Chronos Awards; Davitt Awards). Her ghost/crime story *Jane* won the Athenaeum Library's 'Body in the Library' prize at the 2017 Scarlet Stiletto Awards.

Narrelle's work includes vampire novels, erotic spy adventures, het and queer romance, traditional Holmesian mysteries, and Holmes/Watson romances *The Adventure of the Colonial Boy* (2016) and *A Dream to Build a Kiss On* (2018). Her queer paranormal thriller-romance, *Ravenfall*, was released in 2017. Upcoming books include her short story collection, *Scar Tissue and Other Stories*, due later in 2018, and spec-fic het romance, *Grounded*, to be published in March 2019 with Escape Publishing.

On Patreon, Narrelle is writing novellas in the Duo Ex Machina series of M/M romance crime novellas. The third in the series, *Number One Fan*, is currently being serialized for her supporters.

Website:	www.narrellemharris.com.
Blog:	www.narrellemharris.com
Patreon:	https://www.patreon.com/NarrelleMHarris
Twitter:	https://twitter.com/daggyvamp
Facebook:	https://www.facebook.com/NarrelleMHarris.Writing/
Instagram:	https://www.instagram.com/narrellemharris/
Goodreads:	https://www.goodreads.com/author/show/752016.Narrelle_M_Harris
Amazon:	https://www.amazon.com/Narrelle-M.-Harris/e/B001JP8LB0/

Five White Stones

J. P. Reedman

The cavalcade approached the gates of York. Trumpets blew a mighty blast that reverberated off the ancient walls with their slate-capped watch-towers and stalwart Roman foundations. Banners flapped in the northerly wind, showing a bear and ragged staff – symbols of the Earls of Warwick. Other flags bore his arms and yet others his motto, *Vix ea nostro voco*, which meant 'I can scarcely call these things our own.' However, the Lord Warwick called many places in the north his own, including the castles of Middleham and Sheriff Hutton.

It was to Middleham that young Richard of Gloucester had been sent shortly after his brother Edward's assumption of the English throne. He was to learn knightly arts under the Earl of Warwick's tutelage as befitting a youth who was also a royal duke – and who had recently been created Governor of the North and Constable of Corfe and Gloucester castles, positions that were, of course, in name only until he reached his majority. Still, quite the birthday present for a lad of ten!

But today, Richard, riding in Warwick's cavalcade, did not have to worry about his lessons at Middleham, the hours of practice with wooden swords that left him bruised and weary, the hours of acting as a page to Warwick, refilling his cousin's goblet all night until he thought his eyelids would droop shut and he would fall asleep on his feet.

Today Warwick was entering York on business and he had brought a bevy of young squires and pages along in his company. Although he expected the customary services and manners from those under his care, he implied that he would not look askance if the boys viewed the delights of the city, as long as they did not make nuisances of themselves.

Richard was both excited and apprehensive. He had never visited York before, but had heard tales of its mighty Minster and grand streets – but it was known for its Lancastrian leanings. His father's head had once decked the gate-tower of Micklegate after the battle of Wakefield – alongside that of Richard's brother Edmund, aged only seventeen. They were long gone, of course; Edward had ordered the heads removed after his victory at Towton and placed with their bodies at the Dominican priory at Pontefract, but still the memory remained, even if the horror was no longer visible.

As it was, Richard would not have to witness the site of his dead father's humiliation. Warwick's route into the city was through another of its many 'Bars' – Bootham Bar.

'You look serious.'

Robert Percy, one of Richard's friends from Middleham, glanced towards the youthful rider at his side. He was almost seven years older than Richard and seemed, in Richard's eyes, almost a man. While Richard was still, in his tender years, a page, Rob was a squire to Warwick and helped look after his armour and his horses when he was in residence. For the rest of the time, it was his job to prepare the pages for their future positions as squires – when they were not with the grammar master or being taught chess or dancing.

Richard sighed.

'I was just thinking ... about York ...'

Rob immediately knew what the boy meant and would not say.

'Don't think,' he admonished with a grin. 'You think too much, Richard. We are going to have a splendid time, as long as his lordship the earl lets us out of his sight!'

'Do you think he will?'

Rob winked; he had bright blue eyes beneath a thatch of gleaming dark hair.

'Oh, going on past times, I think so. Warwick believes a youth should see the world and not be overly sheltered. Christ's teeth, you should know he doesn't believe in coddling – he lets us swim in the Black Dub behind the castle, doesn't he, and go off to explore the Old Castle of Red Alan ... all places where you might well be snatched away by a wandering Scot.'

Richard made a face at Rob. 'There are no Scots in Yorkshire.'

'No?' Rob's brows rose. 'Well, there were once. They even made it to York. Tried to capture Queen Isabella who was in town ...' He fell silent. The queen he spoke of was reputed to have been the lover of Roger Mortimer, one of Richard's own ancestors. Roger had virtually ruled England in the minority of Edward III, Richard's royal ancestor in two lines, but had been hung as a common criminal on Tyburn Tree ... 'It was a long time ago,' he finished lamely.

'I know,' said Richard. He had heard the story, but it hardly concerned him. A family of high standing always had so many deaths; Mortimer's was too long ago for emotion. Even his grandfather, Richard of Conisbrough, was from a time before his birth. Only his father's death at Wakefield remained raw, but he endeavoured to hide it well ...

The party entered beneath the frowning barbican of Bootham Bar, riding sedately under the spiked portcullis. Once inside, the red-clad worthies of the town emerged to greet the Lord Warwick, who rode at the head of the company on a grey destrier, his crimson cloak blowing behind him in the wind.

'I hope all the niceties don't go on too long,' murmured Rob, as the mayor, Thomas Scawby, and the local sheriff made welcome speeches to the Earl of Warwick.

His attention was suddenly drawn by a movement in one of the cobbled lanes that snaked off the main street. 'Richard, look! They are going to have a pageant for the earl.'

Richard craned his head around to stare. Out from the lane danced a troupe of mummers. The foremost, wearing feathered bird-masks, played flutes and banged tabors. Behind them strode an antlered man with a crumhorn, his cat-headed companion squealing on bagpipes. At their heels wandered a bear, furry and shambling – not a real bear from the bearpits, but a man in a shaggy skin wearing a wooden head filled with serrated iron teeth. Two other mummers poked and prodded at the bear; both were dressed as knights from a bygone age, one in a blood-red tabard and the other in black, with great feathered plumes waving upon their helmets.

The black knight swaggered forward, taking in the crowd.

Arthgallus, am I, knight of the Round Table,
I defend my liege lord whenever I am able!
My name means 'the Bear' like that of my lord –
I'll smite all other Bears with my trusty sword!

Drawing a pretend wooden sword from the sheath at his belt, he made a dash at his fellow in the bear costume, pretending to whack the creature soundly on the nose.

Richard and the rest of the company burst into laughter, especially the younger members.

While the Bear cowered behind the musicians, Arthgallus stepped forward once more, twirling his long moustaches – a bristle made of horsehair.

Warwick I am, first earl of that name,
Courteous to knave, knight and dame.
I come to welcome he who now bears Warwick's
mighty staff …

A series of ribald titters broke out, and even Warwick, arms folded, was grinning with mirth.

And at the same time, make you laugh!

With a flourish and a deep bow, Arthgallus slunk into the background, behind the still-playing musicians.

Another actor took his place – the knight wearing the red tabard, which was exactly the same shade as Lord Warwick's own livery.

'I am Morvidus, ancestor of *all* the Lords of Warwick!' he cried in a booming voice.

Arthgallus was my doughty son,
But I was first to make the Great Bear run!
I will make you afraid, I will make you laugh.
I will beat the fearsome Bear with the Ragged Staff.

The black knight reappeared and threw him a large, knobbly oak staff decorated with garlands of flowers. The Bear uttered a ferocious growl and pounced upon him, knocking off his helmet. Entwined, the two actors rolled on the ground, while the crowd laughed and catcalled. Then the knight took the staff and proceeded to buffet his opponent. The Bear, clutching its sore head, made a mewling noise like a little kitten and darted behind the musicians to hide as the children in the crowd pelted it with pebbles and twigs.

'Well done, well done all,' said the Earl of Warwick as the pageant finished, the musicians dancing in circles around the Bear, which began to dance too, waving its clumsy arms in the air. 'But now I must attend to business at the Guildhall.'

Warwick remounted his horse and his cavalcade proceeded on its way. Richard glanced back over his shoulder. The crowds around the mummers were dispersing, and he saw the smallest of the musicians remove the mask from her face. Below was a pretty maid about Richard's own age ... but not only was she pretty, she was striking and unusual. There was no colour in her. She was like a girl wrought of the snow that fell on the high moors in winter. Her hair, braided with tiny blue flowers, was white, and no redness dappled her cheeks. She glanced up, perhaps sensing that someone was looking in her direction, and Richard saw that her eyes were the palest shade of blue, the hue of a winter's sky after a thin rain.

She smiled shyly at him and then pushed in amidst the older actors in the troupe.

Rob Percy had seen everything. Surreptitiously he nudged Richard with his elbow.

'Yes, she was fair, Dickon ... but aren't you a little young yet? Too young to be following your brother's example.'

Richard went red to his ears. 'My ... my brother is the king!' he spluttered.

Rob flushed and fell silent. It was easy to forget exactly the importance of this thin, smallish young boy, with his set, earnest face. A Plantagenet ... with a brother who had won his crown through fire and blood at Mortimer's Cross and Towton.

'Richard, I should not have said it. I have a stupid loose tongue sometimes. You know I meant no ill.'

'I know,' said Richard, his flare of anger dying. 'It is just ... I ... I ... We can still be friends, can we not?'

'Of course, as admitted, I spoke out of turn. I will allow you to pummel me in sword practice for my punishment!'

Richard grinned. Rob was relieved to see that grin. The young Gloucester was sometimes too serious. For his age, the child had been through much. And now his brother was king and the world opening up for him.

The entourage continued to the Guildhall, where Lord Warwick conducted his business and the young pages and squires did his bidding while he was closeted with the mayor. After it was over, Warwick gestured the youths to him.

'You have served me well today. I promised you all some freedom in this town, which many of you have never seen. Go now, but stay close – pitfalls can happen in even the friendliest of places.'

He turned to Rob, beckoned him closer with a finger.

'You – Percy. Look after Gloucester, without fail. Keep his name secret in the street.'

'He need not call me by my title, my lord!' butted in Richard, earnest and afraid, as if he thought Warwick might keep him bound to his side and make him miss any boyish revelry. 'I always let him call me Dickon!'

Warwick placed his hands on his hips.

'Well, if I can trust you to mind yourself and obey Percy, Cousin Dickon, you may go.'

'I shall!' cried Richard. 'I promise.'

'Then I let you go with your protector.' Warwick nodded seriously to Rob. 'Do not fail me.'

*

The two boys, along with others in the party, quickly headed down the winding alleys known as Snickleways to find some adventure. They ended up in the Shambles, where the fleshers hung meat out on hooks that overhung the gutter, then proceeded to gape in awe at the massive bastions of the Minster, gold lit in the late afternoon sun. Eventually, growing very thirsty, they entered a busy tavern within sight of the Minster and another church called St Michael le Belfrey. Rob brought two mugs of small beer, one for himself and one for Richard; Richard's face crumpled up as he drank, for the beer tasted much fouler than that he had drunk in Middleham.

As twilight descended, covering the sky with a purple pall, the tavern was full to brimming. Rob was a little tipsy and Richard felt uncomfortable, crushed into a corner while men deep in their cups stumbled around, roaring with mirth. One tripped and almost fell on top of him, spilling rank beer over his doublet.

Richard leapt to his feet.

'Rob, I am going back to the Guildhall to meet Lord Warwick.'

Rob's back was to him; he was chatting up a buxom girl with a rosy, eager face.

'Rob!' Richard called again, more stridently.

Robert was not listening. Richard tried to catch his eye, but the older youth was thoroughly engrossed. Annoyed, Richard slipped out of the crowded tavern and sat on the edge of the gutter, the cobblestones jutting into the back of his thighs. It was beginning to rain, a dull drizzle that turned his hair into embarrassing ringlets. He scowled into the gloom.

Suddenly a nearby lane disgorged a whole host of revellers, dancing, singing, laughing, some of them clearly tipsy. They held bright torches to light their way in the new-fallen night; the light splashed across the damp cobbles and illuminated the boy sitting miserably by the gutter.

'And what do we have here?' A man staggered over, holding up his torch. He was tall, with, to Richard, an outlandish accent. His cloak and hat were covered in silver suns and moons. He had a long beard plaited with blue ribbons.

'A lost poppet by the look of things!' A woman with black hair hanging indecently loose over her shoulders joined the bearded man. She smelt of spices and exotic scents. 'Where did you come from, boy?'

He did not want to answer these strangers and crossed his arms defensively. At that moment, a voice piped up, 'He was with the Earl of Warwick's company. I saw him when we performed!'

A small figure pushed through the knot of bodies. Richard stared; it was the little white-haired girl he'd first seen with the mummers when he'd arrived in York! She was cloaked against the cold now, but her hood was back despite the rain, and long, moon-pale tendrils of hair hung free, flying like banners on the breeze.

'It *was* you, wasn't it?' she said. 'I noticed you …You were special. Different.'

The mummers, for that was who the revellers were, crowded around Richard.

'Special, special,' whispered the older woman. 'If our little Eirlys, our little Snowdrop, thinks you are special, then you are! She *knows* things, she does.'

The mummers had now formed a circle. Richard could only see the lane behind, shining dully in the torchlight, through gaps between their legs. It was as if he was surrounded … deliberately.

A pang of unease gripped him. Where were the beadles and the night-watch in this great town? And where was Rob Percy? No doubt still trying to impress the tavern wench …

'You look afraid,' said the dark-haired woman, teeth gleaming white in the descending dusk. 'We won't hurt you.'

'I'm not afraid,' said Richard fiercely. Being afraid was about the worst insult someone could give him.

The mummers burst into laughter. Richard's cheeks burned.

'Then you won't be afraid to come with us,' said the woman. 'Will you?'

The actors were moving off now, and he was caught in the middle of the group, pushed along by swinging cloaks and jostling hands. Some of the mummers began to play on their instruments, drowning the sound of his voice as he yelled at the dark woman and the man with the be-ribboned beard: 'I can't go with you. I have to return to the Lord Warwick! If I don't return … he … he will come searching with armed men, I swear it!'

'Hush.' A little shape brushed against his shoulder. Glancing over, he saw the white girl, Eirlys. 'They won't hurt you.'

'Then tell them to let me go!'

She stared down; fine rain jewelled on her pale eyelashes.

'This is all my fault. I told them you were special. They believe it is lucky to have you here. Just like a talisman.'

'What are you – a witch?' Richard snapped. He immediately felt guilty at his unkindness; the young girl's head drooped and she looked mortified.

'Of ... of course not. But I have always had the ability to ... see things. My mama, God assoil her, said it was a gift, not a curse. That Almighty God blessed me with the Sight.'

'Do you see me going home?' said Richard. 'Back to Lord Warwick? Don't you understand? I cannot stay out here ... even if I wanted to. Which I do not. Warwick will send his men, and it will not go well for your people. I was not lying.'

'Are you so important, then?' she whispered. Suddenly her eyes were glittering. 'I knew you were. I saw it!'

'Be silent, no one is to know. Eirlys, please, get me away from this acting troupe, I beg you.'

She now seemed to realize the urgency of the situation.

'Where are we going?' she called out to the two leaders, dancing on ahead while the pipes skirled and the hurdy-gurdy wheezed.

'Over the hills and far away,' said the bearded man with a laugh. He was swigging from an earthenware flagon.

'Over hill and over dale,' the black-tressed woman joined in. 'And Luck shall come with us!'

'Eirlys ... please ...' Richard dragged on the girl's sleeve. 'I mustn't stay longer. I have to go back!'

Eirlys bit on her lip. 'It is my fault this has happened. I will try my best ...'

The older mummers were crossing a bridge that

spanned the Ouse, a dark hump of stone with the water rushing below. Richard's heart hammered. Soon one of the gates would become visible. Was it curfew yet, or would his erstwhile abductors dance straight on out into the night? Would yelling and shouting bring help or would the guard see him merely as some ill-mannered guttersnipe?

Eirlys tugged on his hand. They were now several paces behind the others, who were still whirling about and tipsily dancing, caught in the light of the feeble, half-dead torches that lit the top of the bridge. 'Jump, Richard, jump while they aren't looking!'

Over the parapet both children scrambled, landing on a muddy ledge below the river. Eirlys grabbed Richard's hand and dragged him under the struts of the bridge and out along the riverbank.

As they both ran, cloaked in darkness, Richard glanced at his strange companion.

'Hadn't you best go back?'

Eirlys shook her head. 'They can wait. They'll beat me, remember, for letting you go. They'll soon all fall down drunk and sleep it off. I'd rather deal with them when they're sober. Then they'll see how foolish they've been.'

The children continued on in the darkness as the rain pattered down. There was no pursuit, though in the distance they could hear music and drunken shouting. All around, shapes moved; once, by a wall, they saw two cowled shapes huddled by a meagre fire.

'Where is this place?' said Richard, thoroughly disorientated. 'Who are these people?'

'The poor and homeless live on the river's edge. They won't harm …' She suddenly stared at his garments, rich though somewhat bedraggled from the damp. Taking off her cloak, she handed it to him. 'Put that on.'

'But you … you will be cold. And you're a girl,' said Richard.

'I'll be fine. Do as I say, for your own sake.'

Richard decided it was best not to argue and

pulled on the cloak. He had scarcely fastened the clasp when an old woman leaning on a stick came stumbling down the path. She wore a ragged shawl, and one of her eyes looked almost luminous in the darkness – there was a white film over it. She halted, seeming to sense someone ahead. Her free hand came out.

'Alms, alms!'

'We're children, we don't have money,' said Eirlys boldly.

'Nothing at all? Not even a penny for an old woman? We cannot even get fish from the rivers to eat no more; the damned monks build fishgarths in 'em. Fishgarths. What do you say to that, young madam, young sir?'

'I– I will make sure the fishgarths get removed one d–day!' stammered Richard.

'Will you now?' The crone shrieked with laughter, then fell into a fit of coughing.

Richard and Eirlys dashed past her on to the waterside path. At length another bridge crossing the Ouse appeared through the darkness. Beyond, the towers of the Minster glowed coldly. Night-birds, or bats, flapped around the pinnacles.

'Go up that street.' Eirlys pointed. 'Don't turn right or left … and you will be back at the tavern where you were.'

Richard moved to leave, but the girl caught his wrist. 'Wait … *wait*. This place is a magic place. Down by the river. Before you go, let me show you.'

Richard wanted nothing more than to go, but he did not want to be churlish after she had helped him. Reluctantly he went to the riverside with Eirlys. An old willow bent over the bank, its boughs streaming in the water like outstretched hair. Overhead, the rain ceased and a pale moon slipped out, its image shivering on the dark waters.

Eirlys knelt by the water's edge, careless of the mud. Reaching into a pouch at her belt, she brought out five white stones. She held them out on her palm, five pieces of quartz as white as her hair.

'It is said,' she breathed in a low voice, 'that when the Matins bells ring in the monasteries and the monks begin the Night Order, if one drops five white pebbles into the Ouse, he will see a reflection from either the past, the present or the future. Will you not try it?'

With some reluctance, Richard took the pebbles. They felt ice-cold despite having been in Eirlys's hand. Further down the river, the Matins bell of St Mary's abbey began a low, deep tolling; the bells of other monastic houses joined in the clangour.

Richard slowly let the pebbles drop into the shallows. *One ... two ... three ... four ... five.*

He stared at the surface of the water, thinking about what he wanted to see. Not the past – too much evil and sorrow lay there. And the present? Well, that he already knew. But the future ...

For what seemed an age, he could see nothing. Then ... a flicker of gold. Or ... or ... what *was* that on the river's swell? Fish swirling round under the surface, lights from the torches along the rail of the nearby bridge? The moon as it rode westward in the heavens?

The nebulous shape was round and resembled a crown with pointed tines ...

He reached out and his fingers touched the water, and the vision vanished instantly, breaking apart in the ripples his hand had made.

'I saw it!' cried Eirlys, voice filled with excitement. 'You ... are you royal?'

He dared not say he was the king's brother. Not there, out alone in the darkness. And he ... he had not seen it *really*, had he? It surely was just imagination ...

'I must go,' he insisted. 'If you think you'll get a beating, well, I'll get an even worse one from Warwick. And it's not even my fault.'

'Your name!' she cried, a shining pale vision in the gloom. 'Your name at least ...'

He was scrambling away from her up the bank towards the road.

'It's Richard ...' he called over his shoulder. 'Richard ... of Gloucester ...' He would not tell her that Gloucester was not his birthplace – that he was, in truth, its duke ...

'Richard! I will remember you ... next you come to York. And you will come back, I know it ... someday. But not with Lord Warwick!'

At her words, a little shiver ran up his spine. It sounded almost like a prophecy, and Eirlys was a strange, fey creature. It was probably all show, though, used to garner coins from the gullible when the mummers' troupe was on the road.

He was glad to be away.

He rushed up the street, conscious of how out of place he looked, running alone, with the midnight sky above and the chanting of monks an eerie distraction in the distance.

Ahead, he spied a figure on the street corner, equally out of place as he was in the unfamiliar town. Blessed Mary be praised, it was Rob Percy! He raced up to him, slipping on the wet cobbles and bashing straight into Rob's legs, almost knocking him over.

The older youth swore, then grabbed Richard by the collar.

'Where the hell have you been? I have been searching everywhere. Warwick would have killed me if anything untoward had befallen you! I was imagining you dead in the river! Royal duke or no, I should beat the stupidity from you, you little dunderhead!'

'I didn't go of my own volition ... and you shouldn't have been chatting up some girl, but looking out for me. Like my cousin, the earl, told you to.'

Rob shut his mouth with a snap. He knew he was at least partly at fault. He calmed himself down.

'I ... I guess it's both our faults. Let's get back to Warwick's lodgings without further delay. I have a feeling there's going to be a thrashing for us both …'

The youths walked quickly together up the night-clad street. Men exited the taverns, more than merry; women in striped hoods glided to and from the rank alleys, beckoning. Rob tried to guide Richard out of their path, but the younger boy was not paying attention anyway.

He was thinking of the River Ouse.

The five white stones.

The golden crown that was – surely – just a trick of his imagination?

About the author

J. P. Reedman was born in Canada but has lived in the UK for more than twenty-five years. She enjoys history, archaeology and travel. An interest in Richard III dating to the early 1980s was re-awoken by the rediscovery of his grave in 2012.

J. P. is now a full-time author, writing fiction about the House of York, little-known medieval women and ancient Britain. Her best-known Ricardian books are *I, Richard Plantagenet* and *A Man Who Would be King.*

Amazon: http://author.to/ReedmanRichardIII
Facebook: https://www.facebook.com/IRichard Plantagenet/
Twitter: https://twitter.com/StoneLord1

Dame Joanne's Talke Thinge

Larner and Lamb

Oure deare Dames and Subjectes, lett Us telleth ye of the tyme We didst attendeth a talkyng thinge, about Us! 'Twas presented by Oure Dame Joanne, across Muddleham Bridge in ye moderne tymes.

We didst choose Oure clothyng to blend in with ye moderne folk, and so We didst weareth a blacke leathern bomb-berr jackette, Oure right tight fittyng denim jeans hose whyche hath caused mannie a dame to swoone (smooths haire downe) and a flatt capp, the whyche We heareth is verily fetchyng in moderne Yorkshire.

Oh (rolls eyes) here cometh Lovell...

'Hail thee, Lovell, what art thou wearyng, manne?'

'Sire! Dickon! Your Grace! ... I thought it best to blendeth in with ye moderne folk!'

'Oh Lovell, We cannot see thee blendyng wearyng THAT!'

'B-b-but Dickon, dost thou liketh not my shinie, blue, flared breeches and my pinke, frillie shirt? And look Dickon! Plat-ye-form soled shoes!'

(Pinches bridge of nose). Dame Joanne didst suddenlie arriveth and asked Lovell if he were attendyng a circa 1970s disk-oh thinge ... Of course, he was not (sighs).

We didst order him right sternlie to changeth his awfulle apparel to a more 'subtle' outfitt. He cameth back in his orange coat, greene plaid trousers and matchyng shoes ... 'twas subtle, for Lovell ... (shaketh hedd).

Dames Jo and Kokomo arrived to picketh us up in the carr thinge with Oure portrait on its door!

We telleth them: 'Look ye here, dames! No curtseying, no "Your Grace" or "My Liege", no swoonyng (though 'tis difficult not to in Oure presence).' (Smooths haire downe). 'We wysh to blend with common folk. We wysh to be inn-cogg-nitto.'

Dame Kokomo then spake up: 'Aye Dickon, and I feel I may say so, that ye do look right common.' (?) 'And thou, Lord Lovell, lookest right fashionable – thou dost looketh like a professor or an intellectual person!'

HA!!

We were seated in a hall, listenyng to Dame Jo, telling of Oure noble deeds and goodly laws, when Lovell whispered to Us.

'I'm going to ask a question at Ye ende.'

'Oh Lovell.' (Frowns). 'Thou knowest where those boyes both went safely, and without harm to theire persons, thou buffoon!'

'No, Dickon, not that,' he whispered. 'I have a more pressing question.'

'Whatever, Lovell.' (Sighs and rolls eyes).

Then, Dame Joanne sayeth: 'So ladies and gentlemen, that concludes our talk. Do any of you have any questions about King Richard III?'

Lovell stood up. (Pinches bridge of nose). But another manne hath raised his hande in the aire and Dame Joanne did asketh him what was his question.

'How could that old crouchback, King Richard, even ride a horse, let alone fight as courageously as you say?'

We glowered at him – he was an ugly little manne with wonkie eyes and a thinne, cruel mouth. He remindeth Us of someone? ... When he saw Us give him Oure stare of disapproval, he didst beginne to quaketh in his boots.

Dame Joanne, who hath seen Oure angry countenance, didst hurriedlie saye:

'Well, Sir, he wasn't actually a hunchback – that's just Tudor propaganda. And he was very fit.' (Smooths haire downe). 'He is known to have been a great warrior and he very nearly got to Henry Tudor and killed him. It was proved in the documentary that was made that he could have ridden, charged and fought fiercely.'

We narrowed Oure eyes at the nasty little manne and he shuffled his feete nervouslie.

Lovell putteth up his hande.

'Yes, you there, Sir, with the orange coat, professor?'

'I am Professor Francis.'

'And what is your question, sir?'

'Well, madam, I would like to know…' (We glower at him right sternlie). 'Where … err … where is the toilet?'

'Oh!' sayeth Dame Jo, rather perplexed. 'Turn left at the end of the corridor.'

Lovell didst giveth her ye 'thumbs up' signe and headed off, followed by the nasty little manne, who was clutching the front of his trousers and pushed in front of Lovell to get to the privy. His neede was obviously urgent!

'Any more questions?' sayeth Dame Jo.

Of course, We felt that We hadst to rescue the dame, so We didst raiseth Oure royalle hand.

'Madam, I have a question.'

'Oh, and what is your name, Sir?'

'Ah, well, I err … I am Ricky, err Ricky Broom.'

'OK Ricky, what's your question?'

'Madam, dost (coughs) … do you think the reconstruction head of King Richard III is accurate?'

(Smooths haire downe).

'Ah, well, my – err, Ricky – I think I would say in reality King Richard III was probably even more handsome.'

We smileth. 'Ah yes, We, I … err … I, I bet he cut a striking figure.'

The talke ended. We sat downe awaiting Lovell. Suddenlie two ladies sittyng behind Us speaketh.

'Ere Jane, 'e looks like 'im, dont 'e, eh?'

We turned around.

'Rickaay innit? You look like 'im!'

'Hmm? Me?' (We tryeth hard to look innocent).

'Yer, you'd look like 'im if you took yer hat orf, you'd be just like 'im, wouldn't 'e, Doreen?'

''E would,' said the exuberant Doreen.

'Take yer att orf, go on Rickaay!! Take it orf,' they chorused.

Just in time, Lovell appeared. He looked serious.

'Si—, err, Ricky pal, don't remove your hatt, you know what the doctor said.'

We looked regretfully at Jane and Doreen, and We thought Lovell wouldst sayeth that We hath a cold.

'If he removes his hat they will escape and multiply by the second.'

Both women let out an ear-piercing shriek, and hastened awaye from Us.

'Oh Lovell, didst thou have to telleth them We hath head lice, manne?'

'Well ... it worked, Dickon, for thou wert nearly rumbled!'

Dame Jo spoke: 'Oh Sire, we know thy haire is healthie, Dame Kokomo knoweth it too!' and they both touched Oure haire affectionately.

We didst cross Muddleham bridge, weary from Oure time travelling. Oure sonne, Edward, ranne to greet Us, with his beste friend, Lennie Lovell, sonne of Lord Lovell.

'Uncle Richard?!'

'Yes, Lennie?'

'My father says he was a hero todaye!'

'Hmm?'

'Yes, he made two ladies think you had nitts!'

(Sighs) 'Yes, well, of course We do not, it was merely to maketh the inquisitive ladies leaveth Us alone.'

'Uncle Richard?'

'Yes, Lennie?'

'I had nitts once ...'

(Rolls eyes) 'Well, Lennie, We really didst need to knoweth that ... get thee awaye, and practise thy archerie with Edward!' Hmmph! Stupid boy! (Shaketh hedd).

We walked to Oure royalle appartments and put on Oure tunic and hose, and decided to lieth on Oure bedd for a whyle, whereupon We didst heareth a sounde whyche didst frighteth Oure verrie soule.

'Rickaay!!'

We sat up quickly! 'Twas yon naughtie dames, Jo and Kokomo!

'Why, my Liege, I hath my nitt comb to banish yon wildlife from thy haire!' sayeth Dame Jo, laughyng!

'And I shalle calleth thee by thy newe name, Ricky Broom!' sayeth naughtie Kokomo! 'Since thou art "in-cog-NITT-o!"'

'Oh, you both are right naughtie dames! We shalle ... We shalle chase ye around Oure herbe garden and whosoever We catcheth shalle weareth this awfulle capp!'

They squealed and ran as We gave chase.

'I'd rather have thy crown, Sire!' shouteth Dame Kokomo.

'I loveth well thy enormous jewels, too!' yelleth Dame Joanne.

'Get ye hence, ye awfulle dames! We cometh after ye with thys nitt-filled capp!!'

Ah, such funne ... how welle We loveth Oure lyff in Muddleham ...

About the authors

Susan Lamb is fascinated by Richard III. However, so much is written about the tragedies in his life and his demise that she wanted to imagine some lighter moments. When she saw what a huge female fan base he has, the 'Dickon for his Dames' Facebook page came into being.

Susan lives in the West Midlands with her husband, Ray, her mom, and Beauty, the perfectly named greyhound. She loves reading, writing short stories, horses and also visiting historical places connected with King Richard.

Joanne Larner, the 'other half' of Larner and Lamb, is the author of a trilogy of novels about Richard III. She enjoyed reading the Facebook page 'Dickon for his Dames' and so, when Susan asked if she would be interested in collaborating with her to write a book based on it, she jumped at the chance. *Dickon's Diaries*, a madcap mix of medieval and modern, was born and the 'Dames' have now also published *Dickon's Diaries 2*.

Amazon: https://www.amazon.co.uk/dp/B01N2Y4KPM
Facebook: https://www.facebook.com/Dickiethird/
Blurb: https://www.blurb.co.uk/b/7690403-dickon-s-diaries
https://www.blurb.co.uk/b/8808709-dickon-s-diaries-2

Bowyer Tower

Wendy Johnson

My fate, so fragile, so slender, is finally sealed. Fear? I am past fear. Fear was the grip of the Constable's men, bruising my flesh; leading, half-dragging me to this place of confinement. They need not have dragged me. *Would* not have dragged me had it not been for my defiance, my struggles, my cries for justice. The slamming of the door, the screeching of the bolt, the silence that followed; therein dwelt my fear. Gut wrenching, mind rending fear. But that sensation has long outlived its purpose, for what is the use of fear when what will come, will come? I am imprisoned and alone. Alone in my sanity, whilst those around me melt in their madness, dripping servile wax to seal the deed.

The woman. They weep for the woman, hanged at my command, like Judas from his elder tree. They have no thought, it seems, for her crime: for the Kingmaker's daughter and my new-born son, both lapped in lead in Tewkesbury vault. No, the world sees only an outline of the truth. A hurried sketch in palest ink, calling for the artist to fill in the gaps. Except that he never will. This treacherous likeness is how my brother would have me be remembered. And like any other traitor, I am doomed to die. The end will not come by the noose, nor by the knife. No hanging or drawing for the brother of the king. I have been granted that. A mercy? I hardly know. The end will be the end, regardless.

I know that Mother has implored him; her praying hands draped with Paternoster beads. Relentless Mother: chip, chipping away. *He is your brother, Edward, do not spill his blood.* I pitied her divested pride, the long hours upon her knees. I pitied Dickon, too, with his solemn eyes, his efforts at reason. Pitied them both, that they should be forced to plead: that with Edward blood should filter so thinly, while syrup and honey ooze.

My destiny, and my father's, both conjured by a queenly hand: his by war, mine by the lightness of a whisper, a persistent drip-dripping of hate. The rain barrel will overflow if there are storms enough.

Mother and Dickon have had their wish: clemency of a kind, from Edward the king – when his queen had turned her gilded head, and he and I were brothers again. It shall be quick, he has conceded. Quick and unexpected. Shall it be a pillow, then, in the night? Shall I suffocate amongst linen and feathers, my final gasp drowned by quills and down?

Farewells: a courtesy Edward has not refused. His own was taken in the Painted Chamber, a theatre of law, where it was waxed and sealed and tied with tape: no time for privy words. With Mother, there were prayers – the best way, she said, to pass the time. She has left me *Mechtild* for company; her *Book of Ghostly Grace* to see me through the night.

Margaret, I said. I should have liked to have seen Margaret. Mother's beads found their way into my palm; cool and smooth and slithering. *For Margaret's sake. Instead of Margaret. A little comfort.*

And Dickon, united at the end as we were in the beginning. Fortune's Wheel, I told him: it never stops turning. He offered to pray with me too, but I told him Mother had ruined my knees, tried to make him smile, couldn't bear the depths of his sorrow. The ship, I told him, remember the ship across the Narrow Seas, one stormy night in the middle of winter? Told him we shall both wash up together, in another harbour, one day.

Weak February light is fading across Tower yard. The scrape of steel, as the watch is changed, the low, brusque voices of the guards. And the smell of the chamber creeping in as the night settles; old stone, cold stone, like the stone of Tewkesbury vault. I shall know it well, soon enough.

A chink of keys, the rolling of bolts, the glare of a lighted torch. They offer me a goblet; sweet Malmsey, to ease and to calm. Rich and red, its sanguine depths reflect my rippling face: a mirror into eternity.

I drink deeply; feel the trail of wine, from gullet to belly, trickling, scorching, while the gaoler averts his gaze.

Edward's parting gift: a poisoned chalice.

In realisation, I close my eyes, seek Mother's faithful beads:

Pater in manus tuas ... Father into thy hands ...

The chamber is lengthening, stretching away. I rise; unsteady, lurching, my numbed limbs following the widening arc. Beneath my feet, stone gives way to earth, to soil ... to grass ... to green grass ... soft and fresh and drenched with dew.

In the passing of a moment, I am free…

About the author

Wendy Johnson has a passion for medieval history and has been fascinated by the fifteenth century, and Richard III in particular, since childhood. She is a keen amateur writer and was a finalist in the *Woman and Home* Short Story Competition in 2008 with a story set in fourteenth-century York.

Along with her husband, Dr David Johnson, Wendy was a founding member of Philippa Langley's *Looking for Richard Project*, which successfully located the lost grave of King Richard in August 2012, and is a co-author of *Finding Richard III: The Official Account*. Wendy's other historical interests include the Angevin kings of England and the English Civil Wars of the seventeenth century. She is currently researching and writing a historical novel, set during the Wars of the Roses, which is intended to form part of a trilogy. Wendy lives in York, Richard III's favourite city.

Website: http://revealingrichardiii.com/index.html
Amazon: https://www.amazon.co.uk/Finding-Richard-III-Official-Account/dp/0957684029

Ave Atque Vale

Frances Quinn

On a splendidly draped ornate bed in a gloomy room of the palace, Henry VII lay struggling to breathe. Surrounded by whispering ministers and chanting clergy he fought against the quinsy and consumption, and lost. He closed his eyes, and died . . .

. . . He opened his eyes again on to a leaden overcast sky, and realized he was lying prone on coarse grass. Struggling to stand up, a sudden weight dragged him forward and he stared at the heavy chains that shackled his wrists. Raising his hands to study the fetters, he saw they were made of solid gold, set thickly with gems. They were very, very heavy.

Baffled, Henry turned his gaze to his surroundings.

All around him stretched a dreary moorland, reed-grasses hissing in the wind under a grey sky. Here and there huge rounded stones dotted the landscape and in the distance there was a dark smudge that might have been mountains. There was no sign of life in the desolate landscape, not human, animal or bird.

Close by stood a group of the huge stones, with the glint of water between them. He went to make his way towards them and discovered that golden chains bound his feet as well.

Stumbling and cursing, he dragged himself over to the stones and sat down heavily. There was a small pool of peaty-brown water between the stones, rippling in the breeze, reflecting the monotonous sky.

Where was he?

He remembered the deathbed, and the darkness . . .

His thoughts were interrupted by the sound of hoofbeats, and he stood up, peering around him for the source.

Across the sere grasses, a figure on horseback was approaching. As it came closer it resolved itself into a man on a white horse, both in full battle-armour, caparisoned in red and blue and gold.

The rider reined in before Henry, who saw the man lacked a helmet, although in full harness otherwise.

Leaning forward in the saddle, the knight smiled and said,

'Well, Tydder, this is a strange place to meet!'

Henry looked up into the face of Richard Plantagenet, third king of that name, and crossed himself – or tried to: the chains pulled his hand down.

'Saints preserve me! So I am in Hell!'

'Nay, not Hell, but Purgatory. This is where we wait until . . .'

'Until we are cleansed of sin. Aye,' Henry snapped, 'I know my catechism as well as you do, Gloucester. No doubt that is why I am wearing these.'

He held up his shackled hands.

'And what is your penance, then? Eternal saddle-sores on that nag? Or is it one of your cronies transformed for his sins?' He chuckled nastily. 'Lovell, mayhap?'

The destrier stretched its head forward, ears back and eyes rolling. Henry flinched back.

Richard reined in the stallion.

'Peace, Master Surrey,' he said, patting the beast's neck. 'No, this is White Surrey himself. I think the poor creature felt guilty about unseating me, so he followed me here. Lovell escaped your hounds, Henry. You would be amazed at who slipped through your grasping fingers. No, I am fated to ride through this land till I find the path out. I have faith that I will – one day.'

'Hah!' Henry snorted. 'It may be a long while

before you leave this place, Gloucester. There are a scant few folk left to pray for you!'

'Not so.' Richard dropped his gaze to Surrey's mane, one hand playing with the coarse white hair. 'There are still some faithful souls who hold to the truth, despite all the lies you have spread, Tydder.'

'Very few, and growing fewer, I think!'

'Aye, well, your habit of murdering anyone who dared to speak well of me has reduced their numbers, certainly.'

'Traitors all!' Henry snapped. 'They threatened my throne, the succession!'

'Children and old women? *Your* throne?' Richard glared at him, then sighed. 'There's naught I can do about that now. You and I must complete our penance, Tydder, and trust in God's mercy.'

'Amen to that!' Henry sat back on his stony seat. 'But,' he said, smiling thinly as a thought struck him, 'I may not be here to keep you company for very long, Gloucester.'

'How so?'

'I have left instructions in my will for thousands of masses to be said for me, prayers in perpetuity, and each one will hasten me out of this place. I will say farewell to you now, and let you continue your endless quest. I will not see you again, I trust.'

'Ah, Henry, Henry.' Richard shook his head. 'I fear you will bear me company a while yet. All your chantries and churches and abbeys are gone, along with your masses and prayers.'

'What?' Henry said, aghast. 'You lie, Gloucester! Ever the false, usurping –'

'Usurping? You would know more of that than I! But I do not lie. Look into the waters beside you, and see I speak the truth.'

Henry did as he was bidden.

The dark waters rippled, showing only the dull sky. Then he saw shapes – becoming clearer, so it was like looking through a window.

He saw roofless churches, abbeys demolished, the stone carted away to build manors and walls.

Sacred vessels melted down, statues broken, paintings destroyed.

Stained glass windows smashed and scattered.

Priests and nuns made homeless, wandering the roads. An elderly abbot cruelly executed.

The poor and sick left helpless, no hospitals or charity left to them.

'In God's holy name! What has happened? Has there been an uprising? A war?'

Henry turned to Richard, who crossed his hands on the saddle-bow and shrugged.

'Time here runs on a separate path to that in the world we left. While you have been here, your mother has died and your son has done this. Your son, Henry. Your second-born son, who has caused it all because he cannot think with what is between his ears. He has condemned you – and his grand-dame – to a longer time here. Almost I could feel sorry for you.'

Henry looked back to the pool where images continued to flicker across the surface.

'My mother?' he whispered.

'Yes, she is here, too,' Richard said, gesturing at the empty land. Then he ducked his head as a large black and white bird swooped at him out of nowhere and flapped across to perch on Henry's shoulder.

The magpie croaked and fluttered its wings.

'And a pleasure to see you again, Dame Beaufort,' Richard said acidly, 'and looking better than I have seen you in many a year!'

Henry flinched as the bird settled its grip on his shoulder.

'Mother?' he said, weakly.

'You cannot tell, Henry? Surely her countenance has not changed that much?' Richard looked very close to laughter. 'But now, I must say my farewells. Much as I would like to stay and talk of old times, I have my own way to find. *Ave atque vale*, Henry!'

Bowing in the saddle, Richard turned Surrey's head and set off across the wide moors.

Henry Tydder sighed.

He turned to the magpie, which had hopped on to the stone beside him.

Now that he looked at the bird, it did remind him of his mother – especially around the eyes.

He looked back at the retreating figure of Richard Plantagenet, and saw the clouds above the rider suddenly part. A ray of bright sunlight enveloped the man and horse, flaring off the armour. As abruptly as it had opened, the cloud cover rolled back, returning the gloomy sky to a dead grey – and showing an empty landscape.

Coming to a decision, Henry began to dig in the soft earth beside the pool, pulling up loose, fist-sized stones and stacking them into a neat pile.

Perhaps it would be a long wait, but he was determined to give his stupid son a right royal welcome. . .

About the author

Frances Quinn lives in Dublin, Ireland in a house filled with books, antlers and art supplies. A self-taught artist who occasionally dabbles in writing, her interest in Richard III dates back to the early 1980s when she read Josephine Tey's *The Daughter of Time.*

Examples of Frances' art can be found on the Internet at DeviantArt.com and on her Facebook page.

Website: https://www.deviantart.com/echdhu
Facebook: https://www.facebook.com/theArtofFrancesQuinn/

Buckingham's End

Richard Unwin

An excerpt from *A Wilderness of Sea*

Laurence, the king's armourer, and a few friends are contemplating the effects of the Duke of Buckingham's rebellion against King Richard and the ambition of one Henry Tudor, titling himself Earl of Richmond.

The denizens of the Bell Inn were noisier than usual, Laurence thought, as he sat in a favoured place by the fire with David Morgan and John Fisher. John's wife, Gurden, was engaged in bawdy repartee with some of her customers, her blithe spirit one of the reasons the inn was highly popular in Gloucester; the other was the quality of the wine and viands. Laurence and David had taken lodging at the inn after resting a mere day at Laurence's forge. He thought on the forge where John Fisher kept the smiths and armourers busy with the orders he continued to send from his contacts at court. The king alone had ordered a huge quantity of arrowheads, halberd blades and spearheads which was enough to keep the forge busy for some weeks. John acted at the forge as Laurence's steward while Gurden ran the inn most efficiently and thus the couple were becoming, if not rich, then comfortably off. Laurence too was quite a wealthy man, especially when he added payment for his work on the king's armour and that of other nobles, with profits lodged in a London banking house.

      Sir James Tyrell arrived, as he always seemed to just when Laurence was most contented, bent on destroying his fond reverie. David and John had been discussing the recent rebellion and wondering at the whereabouts of the perfidious Duke of Buckingham when he strode into the inn. David Morgan, of course, was one of his men, so it was obvious he would have left word where he could be found.

'We have him, the traitor Buckingham,' Tyrell declared triumphantly. 'Hidden away at Wem and given up by a snivelling servant, the man he thought was protecting him. Most fitting for a traitor.'

'Where is he?' said David, jumping to his feet.

'Safe in the gaol here, for now. The sheriff of Shrewsbury has him in charge. Tomorrow we proceed to Salisbury.'

'He will be taken to the king, I suppose?' said Laurence.

'He will not,' snapped Tyrell. 'His Grace will not grant him audience. The traitor Henry Stafford will be given trial at Salisbury, presided over by Sir Ralph Assheton who is appointed by the king, then executed. I have sent advance word to begin constructing the scaffold.' Tyrell, Laurence noted, had corrected his earlier mistake of using the title Buckingham and now reverted to the familial name of Henry Stafford. 'We are to attend upon the king who is on his way to Salisbury. Be ready to leave at first light.'

*

'The wretch is most abject, Your Grace, and begs an audience most humbly,' said Catesby.

King Richard stood firmly, his legs placed for balance as if about to launch himself at a deadly foe. This was partly so that Laurence could check the fit of his armour, and partly in hate for the traitorous duke, his erstwhile friend and chief supporter.

'Tell him he shall have a priest to confess to,' he barked. 'That is all the audience he will be granted from us; his next interview will be with the Devil in the foul pit.'

'Might I ask Your Grace to place himself so?' asked Laurence, striking a martial pose.

King Richard glared at him angrily for a moment, then grumped and copied his armourer's stance. Laurence pulled and pressed around the joints and pleats of the harness, marking with a chalk one or two points he thought might require some work. Though he was concentrating on what was, at this time, a delicate task around the body of the king, yet he took his time the longer to remain in the presence.

'Traitor though he is, he wishes to impart something to Your Grace,' continued Catesby doggedly. 'A secret, the knowledge of which will serve Your Grace.'

'I have no curiosity whatever for anything he has to say to me. You are a lawyer, Catesby, and thus a hoarder of secrets, which are your stock-in-trade, but I have no such interest. I know all I need to of Henry Stafford; he is already dead to me.'

'But there still may be . . .'

'Enough! I shall hear no more.'

'Very good, Your Grace,' said Catesby with a graceful bow. He had pushed the matter of the Duke of Buckingham's plea for an audience with the king as far as he dare. Laurence wondered why he had been so persistent. Perhaps it was, as the king said, the consuming desire of a lawyer to probe secrets. Catesby, however, was not the kind Laurence would trust with any of his secrets. He remembered too well how the disclosure of a certain secret marriage contract, harboured by the lawyer for years, had brought Lord William Hastings to his doom and deprived a boy king of his crown.

'Your squires have maintained the harness in good order, my lord king,' said Laurence. 'There are one or two rivets that might be closed up, but otherwise, unless Your Grace can inform me further, it is fit for battle.'

'That is good. If, as my good Sir William here fears, there are more traitors out there, I shall deal with them with harness on my back, not whisper at them to go away.'

'I only meant . . .' stammered Catesby.

'Well, Catesby, you meant well I know, but I have had enough of treason. It has dogged my footsteps ever since my brother Edward died.'

King Richard sat himself wearily on a stool by the window of his chamber and looked down into the courtyard. They were in the finest room of Salisbury's best inn and the courtyard below was crammed with men-at-arms and others. Some noticed the king at his window and immediately stopped to make obeisance. He gave an impatient wave of his hand to get them to return to their duties. One of the serving men in the chamber brought a goblet of wine from which the king sipped sparingly, in deep thought.

'I remember at the latter wars in Scotland,' he said at length to nobody in particular, 'I was on board ship with Jockey Norfolk.' Laurence smiled at the king's use of the nickname the Duke of Norfolk, John Howard, was fondly known by. 'There was a black storm and we put out to sea, away from the coast for safety. We were surrounded by great waves as far as we could see – a wilderness of sea that, at any moment, might have washed us away. God, in his mercy, delivered us, but I feel now as I did then, surrounded by hostile elements all of which would drown us.'

'Except, Your Grace, on land you can wear good armour to protect you,' said Laurence. 'At sea, the same would drag you down.'

The king turned his head and smiled at him benignly.

'Our thoughts exactly,' he said quietly. 'We would not put out on to a sea of lies and treachery to be dragged down. We shall fight treason dry shod, well armed and with a good conscience.'

'Well said, Your Grace,' responded Laurence.

The king's attention was suddenly drawn to a

commotion in the courtyard below. He stood up and peered down.

'Sir James Tyrell has arrived and seems most anxious,' he said. 'By the looks of him he has a report to make. Give him immediate audience.'

Sir James burst into the chamber in a manner that would normally have brought him a rebuke, but his flushed face and air of excitement had everyone's attention. He knelt before the king, his eyes bright and shining.

'The Tudor's ships have sailed from Brittany, Your Grace. They are expected to be off our coast in a few days, except the weather is not in their favour.'

Richard clapped his hands. 'Let him land! I shall have him when he does and then perhaps the realm may have some peace.'

'I think he will not know Buckingham has failed in his rebellion,' gushed Tyrell.

'Then we must not disabuse him; rather let him believe that Buckingham has won the day. Where is he expected to make landfall?'

'That is difficult to say, Your Grace, given the state of the winds from Brittany,' replied Tyrell. 'I would expect somewhere around the coast of Cornwall . . . perhaps?'

King Richard paced the room, thinking out what was his best course.

'We shall move with the army to Exeter,' he ordered. 'Have the coast watched and report to me there.'

'Rebels are still holding out around Bodmin and Plymouth, Your Grace,' advised Catesby.

'Then we shall deal with them from Exeter,' he declared. 'They will not last long seeing most of their leaders have already deserted them. Sir James, get you hence with your men to Cornwall. See to it they are well armed. Master Laurence, you will go with them and see to their harness.'

'Very good, Your Grace.' Laurence swept the king a low bow of obeisance.

'Oh, and Sir James, see to the arrangements for the execution of the traitor Buckingham before you leave. Sir Ralph Assheton will have pronounced over him by now. I would have him out of this world before we depart for Exeter.'

'Everything is in hand, Your Grace. He will be gone early on the morrow.'

'Give word for my captains to attend upon me,' called the king. Immediately his retainers scuttled around crying for messengers to get word to the nobles in command of the king's army. Laurence and Sir James Tyrell bowed and backed from the king's presence.

*

The sun next morning crept up on a world shrouded behind thin grey cloud. The year 1483 had turned to November with yet much unresolved campaigning to do in spite of the near impossible weather conditions. None of this bothered the Duke of Buckingham as he was brought to the scaffold erected in the market square at Salisbury. The leaden aspect of the skies could hardly be more oppressive than the weight that bore on his soul.

Harry of Buckingham was not ready to die.

Most of his days had been spent at his estates where he oppressed his people and grumbled about his wife, Katherine Wydville, a commoner whom he felt was beneath him. He kept away from Edward's court and had few thoughts on his title to the throne of England, other than the petty jealousy his distant claim might have engendered in his breast. Unlike Henry Tudor, *his* mother had not stirred him to revolt; that was entirely his own doing and he bitterly regretted it now. Why hadn't he remained at Brecon and eschewed Richard's court as he had Edward's?

When Edward died, he realized there was much to

play for. Ever the opportunist plotter, Margaret Beaufort, Lady Stanley, through her friend and fellow conspirator Bishop John Morton, had told him of her plans for her son Henry, and when it was discovered the two sons of King Edward were barred from the succession, suddenly ambition, hitherto but a smouldering scrap within his brain, burst into flame. Lady Stanley it was who put the idea in his head that the two boys might be disposed of to clear the way for another claimant. Of course, the Beaufort woman believed that would be her son, but Buckingham thought he could prosecute his own agenda, fool that he was. He would help Richard of Gloucester to the throne and persuade him to murder the two boys to eliminate any further claim by them. This would turn the people against Richard, which should have made it easy to remove him. Afterwards he, Buckingham, would revoke his support for Henry Tudor and take the throne. That is what should have happened, and it had nearly worked – if only the weather had not turned, or Henry Tudor had made it with his promised army of five thousand. King Richard had recoiled from the suggestion of murder and now the boys were gone to ground. At least the Beaufort woman was confounded in that. What a fool he had been to think he could outwit the subtlest plotter in the realm.

   They shoved him towards the steps of the scaffold. He was unable to control his trembling limbs and tears ran down his cheeks as he heard, somewhere distant, the intonations of the priest they had allowed him. The priest was following behind, hastily brought from the cathedral. Bishop Lionel of Salisbury had been one of the rebels who had fled at the approach of the king. This was a minor cleric, commanded to attend the duke in his last moments. At Wem he had been hiding, disguised as a humble serving man, and the same rags he had been caught in flapped about his cold limbs. All his effort had been taken up by his constant pleading to be brought to the king and he had not thought to ask for his own robes. If only he could throw himself at the feet of the king and explain how foolish he had been, put the blame where it rightly belonged on Margaret Beaufort and Bishop Morton. He would retire to his estates and never leave them again, just as he had when King Edward reigned. King Richard would never again hear a single treasonable utterance from Henry Stafford.

The block was before him. They had not even taken the trouble to hide the axe that would separate his head from his body. The axeman, a great hulking fellow, was scowling with contempt as he saw the pathetic duke having to be shoved on to the scaffold. Nobles were very good at condemning others to death and, truth to tell, they mostly met their own bravely.

But Henry Stafford, Duke of Buckingham, was not ready to die.

His contrition was absolute – *the king . . . just let me speak to Richard.*

He felt himself grabbed from behind, his arms pinioned, and now he was being pushed down, his neck on the block. *Please, the king, it wasn't me – my friend, just one word, mercy . . .*

*

'It is fortunate that you two came along,' growled Tyrell, as he, Laurence and the soldier David Morgan rode at the head of his troop of armed men. 'I can never get any sense from those hereabouts, with their confounded cackling.'

Laurence, a Breton who had many difficulties with the variety of English dialects he encountered about the realm, grinned smugly. In and around Cornwall they spoke Breton, or at least a version of it that was close to the language of his homeland, as was Welsh. He and David, as near native speakers, had little difficulty in conversing with the local population. Thus they had discovered the state of the rebellion in the area. Certain rebels were still holding out, though they were confining themselves behind castle walls rather than ranging about the land.

Their leaders, once they had committed to rebellion, had little choice other than to flee the country or stay and brazen it out, hoping, no doubt, for a king's pardon. So it was that they had managed to get towards Plymouth without any resistance. Villages and town streets were devoid of people as they rode through, and where they found an inn for the night, the locals seemed to have suddenly become abstemious regarding their drink and kept to their own firesides.

'Our king, I think, is too free with his pardons,' grumbled Tyrell. 'Folk believe they only have to keep their heads down for a time and no retribution will be visited upon them. King Edward would have made them pay dearly for daring to rise against him.'

'Perhaps King Richard understands how they have been fooled into thinking their king is wont to murder babes as they sleep – that is one of the rumours going about,' offered Laurence. 'Violent retribution among the general population would rather tend to confirm them in that belief.'

'The king acts firmly enough with the leaders, though,' said David. 'Buckingham was shown no mercy whatsoever and Thomas Saint Leger, the husband of the king's own sister, is also taken and due to suffer the same as Buckingham.'

'He takes it badly when treachery involves those in his own family. They suffer most who offend against King Richard's personal motto – *Loyaulté me lie*,' said Laurence. 'Former friendship or family influence is no defence for treason.'

'The expectation locally seems to be that Henry Tudor will come with an army and invade the realm to bring justice and depose one they have been told is a tyrannical king,' mused David.

'Yes, and the area around Plymouth is a likely place, seeing as he comes from Brittany. It was about eighty years ago Bretons captured the town and occupied it for a time,' Laurence informed them. 'The whole coast around here is convenient for the winds that blow from Brittany.'

They rode on the Devon side beyond Plymouth, heading towards Wembury. There were extensive views across the sea and they considered it the best place to look for Tudor's invading ships. For one thing there was a beach there. The wind whipped around them and every man huddled inside his riding cloak with hoods pulled up over their sallets. As they topped the rise above Wembury they could see Plymouth Sound vastly extending to the west and across the sea to the south, their vision disappeared into a grey haze long before reaching a far horizon. A curiously peaked island, nothing more than a rock, rose from the sea as if marking the whereabouts of a convenient landing place.

And there he was, the Tudor! Not, as they had supposed, with a fleet, but just two carracks, one flying the flag of Brittany and the other displaying a red dragon, which Henry Tudor had politically selected as his badge, hoping for support from his uncle Jasper's followers in Wales. The vessels were clearly having great difficulty holding station in the rough sea; though they had ventured near enough to drop anchor, they would not be able to remain there for long.

Tyrell turned to one of his men and sent him off to inform King Richard that they had found Tudor.

'Let us dismount and make our way on to the headland where we can be seen,' suggested Laurence. 'We should keep our mounts out of sight lest they perceive they are dealing with soldiers rather than local rebels. Hopefully we might entice a landing. Once on shore we can invite them inland and move them towards the king's army.'

'Laurence and I can talk to them, in Breton and Welsh. They won't expect to be addressed thus by King Richard's men. It might fool Tudor into coming ashore.'

'By the Virgin, it would be a feather in our caps if we could capture Henry Tudor,' gushed Tyrell, his face alight with the idea. 'Keep our pennons out of sight and cover your livery with your cloaks,' he commanded his sergeant, who promptly ordered the men to dismount and tether their horses safely. Tyrell had thirty armed men in his command, enough to deal with a small force, yet it was not known how many were in the ships. It was unlikely Henry Tudor would come ashore before his soldiers, so subterfuge was their best chance. Once they began to move inland, Tyrell was confident he could at least cut off their retreat when they finally detected the deception. Hopefully the king would have sent reinforcements by then.

They ranged themselves at intervals along the headland in plain view of the ships. Spread out thus they would not appear a disciplined military force. In front of them was a coastal path that led down to the beach.

'I think that David and I should go to the beach as if in expectation of their arrival,' said Laurence. 'If those are Breton soldiers they will be more likely to come ashore if they hear a fellow countryman address them.'

'Good idea,' enthused Tyrell. 'But first, remove your surcoats. Present yourselves plainly and they might come to us.'

Laurence and David shrugged off their cloaks and removed their surcoats, which were coloured murrey and blue and emblazoned with the badge of the white boar. Both had leather jacks beneath, which were suitably restrained in appearance, as would be expected apparel for country rebels. Their riding cloaks were of oiled brown wool and also dour, providing them a degree of anonymity. Thus clad, the two of them tramped down the path and made their way to just above the tide line. The sea was rough and breakers were rolling on to the shore. Any boat trying to get ashore would have much trouble. They wrapped their cloaks around themselves against the biting cold of the wind, and waited, staring out across the breaking waves to the vessels pitching and tossing on the sea. They could just make out the heads of men ranged along the decks and up on the fore- and after-castles.

Presently, one of the vessels lowered a boat and a few men managed to clamber into it and pull for the shore. Laurence guessed the boatmen must be Breton seamen, perhaps fishermen, as only superb boat-handling would get them ashore and then off again. Skilfully the oarsmen in the boat breasted the surging surf and let the bow slide into the shallows, whereupon they leapt out and dragged it partly out of the water. They were, indeed, dressed as rough Breton seamen. Laurence stepped up to them and gave them a hand in securing the boat. He greeted them in Breton and immediately had their attention. He stood back as another, dressed as a noble, clambered out of the boat and stood, somewhat gratefully, on the shore. On closer scrutiny he had the look of a rough soldier about him, though he was dressed in a fine brown leather doublet under a scarlet cloak. A sallet with a rather sad yellow plume covered his head. His hose was dark blue and he wore boots that came almost up to his knees.

'Greetings and welcome to England,' ventured Laurence in Breton.

'Welcome? That is what I am here to discover,' came the arrogant reply, though in the same language. By his accent and manner, Laurence thought he recognized a mercenary captain rather than a court noble. Brittany had many such for hire, and Henry Tudor would probably need quite a few if his invasion was to have any chance of success. However, there were many exiles from England, particularly among the Wydville family and their followers. He had wondered if one of these would come ashore first. Apparently not; it seemed the Tudor wasn't taking any chances.

'Henri Vasson, at your service.' The Breton gave him a perfunctory bow. Laurence responded with a deeper bow. 'Who are you – a Breton?' enquired Henri.

'I am, in the service of Duke Francis the second. I am his agent here in England, Laurence de la Halle.'

David came over and joined them.

'Where is the rest of the fleet?' he asked the Breton.

'Ah, a Welshman, I perceive,' said Henri Vasson. 'My lord, the Earl of Richmond, will no doubt be glad to hear such accents again. As for the fleet, we are dispersed. Unless they find us here we shall not land.'

Laurence felt a pang of desperation.

'But the rebellion – my lord the Duke of Buckingham awaits Henry, Earl of Richmond to continue his march towards London. The king's cause is lost and he has fled north.' Laurence injected a note of urgency, which he hoped would encourage the man to report the fictional situation to his master. He included the Tudor's self-proclaimed title to add legitimacy to his statement.

'The king is beaten, you say?'

'He is, and will remain so if only we can consolidate our gains; to do that we need my lord of Richmond with us. The people will rally to his banner.'

Henri Vasson gazed up at the men standing casually on the headland. 'Who are these?' he said, sweeping an arm to encompass Tyrell's men.

'They are followers of William Collingbourne,' replied Laurence hurriedly. Collingbourne, a name he knew from Cornelius, had been in contact with Henry Tudor in Brittany and was one of those attempting to get him to invade England. He expected the Breton mercenary would know the name too.

'Collingbourne? I had not been told he was to meet us here.'

'We had no clear idea where you would appear. There are other followers of Buckingham along the coast. It just so happens that here is where Collingbourne's men are placed.' The mercenary looked up at the men on the headland, carefully considering what he had heard. 'I must impress upon you the need for all speed, otherwise the king will have time to reform his army. If we act quickly we can be in London within a week.'

'We are too few,' muttered Henri, half to himself.

'We should wait for the others in our fleet.'

'Henry Tudor is worth ten thousand or more should he land and meet up with Buckingham,' responded Laurence enticingly. 'His mother, Margaret Beaufort, the lady Stanley, is poised to bring her husband's men into the cause. She only waits upon her son.'

At the name of Lady Stanley the Breton mercenary made up his mind. The fact he was conversing with one of his own countrymen along with a Welshman encouraged him to believe them. The other Tudor, Jasper, had lands in Wales and he knew they were expected to gain much support there.

'Very well, I shall convey your news to the earl. First, I will take a closer look at those men on the headland. I need to know we are sufficient in number to make our way inland.'

He began the tramp upwards by the rough pathway. Laurence tried to think of something to dissuade him without making it look suspicious, but was unable to do so. He exchanged a glance with David whose face remained passive, indicating they had little choice. He hoped Tyrell would have enough time to get all signs of identification off his men before they encountered the mercenary.

They could tell by Tyrell's facial expression that he had no idea how to respond to the presence of the man Laurence and David were bringing to him. Those of his men close to him had either removed their surcoats or had wrapped themselves in their cloaks to prevent identification as the king's men.

'This is Captain James,' said Laurence by way of introduction. 'He commands Collingbourne's men.' A flicker of confusion passed over Tyrell's face and Laurence hoped the mercenary had not noted it. 'May I present Monsieur Henri Vasson, one of the captains in the army of our lord, the Earl of Richmond?'

Tyrell, catching on, swept the Breton a bow.

'I am relieved you have come at last,' he managed to get out.

'Monsieur Henri wishes to know our strength before he will report to the earl it is safe to land.'

'I understand,' said Tyrell brightly. 'We are thirty armed men in all, a useful number when added to your men in the ships.'

'Are they well accoutred?' said Henri, speaking in English while looking at the man nearest to Tyrell. All were cloaked against the wind that roared across the headland from the sea, obscuring their weapons. Tyrell nodded at one of his men.

'Open your cloak and show the captain your weapon,' he ordered. The man complied and fortunately he was one who had removed his surcoat. The Breton examined his cuirass and tugged at the man's belt, noting the sword and dagger he carried there.

'These are light arms to fight a king's army with,' declared Henri.

'We have our horses tethered nearby along with our spears and axes,' drawled Tyrell. 'We hadn't thought to greet the Earl of Richmond armed to the teeth.'

'No, perhaps not.' Henri surveyed the men before him and looked towards those ranged along the headland. 'And where is King Richard right now?'

'Chased away into Scotland,' blurted out Tyrell before Laurence could answer.

'That's right,' he interrupted before Henri could ask Tyrell any more questions. 'His queen is at Lincoln and from there he will get up to Middleham, then hence to Scotland.'

Henri Vasson kept his face straight, betraying nothing of his thoughts. If he suspected their story was being hurriedly concocted, he was not showing it.

'I think I have seen enough,' he grunted with a nod of his head. 'If I might go back to the beach, I shall return to the Earl of Richmond and recommend he comes ashore.'

Laurence put out an arm, steering him towards the pathway. He hoped that the Breton had not noticed the brief flash of triumph in Tyrell's eyes at his words.

They stumbled their way down the rough pathway and walked across the tide line to where the ship's boat was located, its stern bobbing up and down as each wave broke on the sand. Henri Vasson walked with Laurence by his side while David Morgan trailed somewhat behind. Henri shouted to his men to ready their oars. Two shoved the boat into the sea and held it while Henri stood, his boots awash and one hand on the gunwale ready to leap aboard.

'I know little of English affairs, my friend,' he said with a wry smile, 'but one thing I do know: Richard Plantagenet will hardly be welcome as an exile in Scotland having been the one who has subdued that nation.'

'Captain James is hardly in a position to know King Richard's plans,' responded Laurence desperately. 'We should not take his words too literally.'

'Yes, I think I agree with you. Perhaps we shall meet again, in our homeland?'

With that he swung his legs over the gunwale of the boat and his oarsmen leapt aboard with him. Together they backed water and managed to turn the boat bow in to the waves. Soon they were pulling beyond the breakers at the beach and heading for their ship. Laurence and David looked disconsolately at each other, both feeling a hollow sinking of their hopes.

Tyrell was furious when he saw the ships make sail and set off across the grey wilderness of sea, clearly heading away from England.

'You have let the Tudor slip through your fingers,' he railed at Laurence.

'I believe it was you who mentioned Scotland thoughtlessly,' he retaliated.

'Why did you have to tell him the king had fled to Lincoln? If you had left the talking to me we would have the Tudor in our grip by now.'

'Since when did you speak Breton?' retorted Laurence.

Tyrell clenched his fists and, raising his arms, shook them furiously at the rapidly vanishing vessels. David Morgan was standing behind his master, not in a position to argue in Laurence's defence, but simply gestured with a hopeless shrug only Laurence could see. Presently Tyrell stamped away to where the horses were tethered, followed closely by David. The rest of the men came down from the headland ready to form up and follow their captain, each one glad that he was not the one who must make report of Tudor's escape.

Laurence stood alone on the headland and looked out across the stormy seas. The Breton vessels could hardly be seen now as they merged into the murk that obliterated the horizon. At least Henry Tudor had been driven away from England, his attempt at invasion in tatters. Hopefully his ambition would soon assume the same condition and England might live in peace under its rightful king. He felt a tight drawing of the scar on his face as the rain began to strike, driven across the land by the wind that had come from Brittany. The thought came to him that England, too, had received some scars in dispute with the Tudor, whose insignificant and bastard claim to the throne had brought such misery, and left a prince exiled anonymously abroad in fear of his life. He turned and trudged through the hillocks that backed the beach. It seemed to him at that moment his future was as bleak as Henry Tudor's. The two women he loved most in his life were lost to him, yet he still had a son from each of them. Perhaps now, under a king whose rule promised to be based on equity and justice, and with the Tudor gone, they could rest more easily. For sure, after the latter wars England needed a time of peace. He might go home to Brittany, a thought he instantly dismissed. His business was here in England and this is where he would remain, at least until his boys were grown and secure in their lives.

Suddenly, a blinding flash illuminated the sky

followed by a long, rolling growl of thunder that shook the very air. He raised his damaged face to the clouds, seeing them sweep in from the sea, dark and menacing. He crossed himself and, searching beneath his cloak, found the reliquary at his neck. Grasping it in his fingers, he prayed to St Barbara, protector from lightning strike and patron saint of armourers.

About the author

Richard Unwin is a retired technical author who lives in Manchester, England. He has written a series of fictional books set in the Middle Ages with a strong Ricardian theme. As a member of the Manchester branch of the Richard III Society, he has written and given talks on themes set in the fifteenth century with a particular interest in examining and debunking orthodox historical verisimilitude.

Richard's non-fiction works include an analysis of the bones in the urn at Westminster Abbey, supposedly the remains of two Plantagenet princes, a short biography of the eighteenth-century ironmaster John Wilkinson, and a critical look at the life of the Elizabethan spy, Christopher Marlowe.

Website:	http://www.quoadultra.net/
Amazon:	https://www.amazon.co.uk/Richard-Unwin/e/B0045XWWMM

Abduction

Joanne R. Larner

Eddshiran's skin flushed a deep red, his angry gaze burning into them.

'This is the start of a very important phase of the research mission and you are not taking it seriously enough.' He turned his eyes towards the tallest one. 'Broonomarz, if you will not obey my directives, it will be the time-loser for you. Oh yes, the time loser it will be.'

'I take your directives most seriously, Monitor Eddshiran. It is just that I fear we may be interfering too much in the aliens' life pathway.' His skin flushed red, then olive. 'We have taken and examined over one thousand of the yellowheads and almost as many brownheads and blackheads. We even have several orangeheads. The Dominion must have found out everything there is to know by now. Why do we need to take more? And now we are told we must take some juveniles back home to study and never release them back to their clans. It seems harsh.'

'To question the Dominion's orders is not your place.' Eddshiran paused and looked down at the ground while they waited quietly. 'However, since you do so, I will inform you of the reason. Our life-giving odour is becoming less and less concentrated. You have surely noticed our powers are becoming depleted?'

'Of course, but the aliens have no such powers.'

'No, although we have found small traces in some of them – those who have a diet high in what they call "fish". The scientists think they can isolate the active molecules, but we must use specimens with the strongest life force we can find, which are the juveniles!' His cold, bloodshot eyes narrowed as he stared at each of them in turn. 'So, this is your last warning! And you too, Bayonsay, Dollipartonn. I have been too soft with you, too soft, I say. Well, no more. You must take two yellowhead juveniles this night and we shall take them home to Orbb, along with the brownheads, orangeheads and blackheads we already have. Two of each as the Dominion has said. You are dismissed – dismissed, I say!' He flicked his antennae at them irritably.

The three Moins waved their feelers in the air in a gesture of respect and obedience and withdrew from the chamber of their Honourable Monitor, progressing backwards, smoothly gliding until they were outside the perimeter and the gateway slid shut with a whoosh of liquid.

'Well, we got away with it that time, we did,' said Bayonsay. He had turned an unhealthy bright yellow whilst they had been undergoing Eddshiran's reprimand. Even Broonomarz, the bravest of the three, was a pale lemon colour. 'We must be more careful in the future, more careful. They will accept no more excuses. We must obey the directive now, we must. I do not wish to go in the time-loser. Last time I lost five Orbb centuries, I did.'

'You are right, I suppose,' said Broonomarz. 'I, too, wish not to lose any more of my time. The aliens are not so important that we should sacrifice life-time.' His tentacles writhed as he wrestled with his misgivings. 'I still think it is not right, though, not right. They are living creatures, even if they are quite repulsive.'

His skin turned a little green as he pictured them.

'I have studied them here for decades already and got to know a little of their ways. They are totally savage and warlike, and yet strangely they do bear a great love for their children. Our actions will cause much suffering, much suffering.' He shook both his heads sadly.

'So where should we go to find the two juvenile yellowheads, where?' Dollipartonn wiggled his heads questioningly. 'The rival Moin-clans have already got their quota of black, brown and orangeheads. We are late, we are! We should try to get some really good specimens.'

'We should fly down to the most populated community and then we will have more choice, so we will.'

'In that case we must don our light-absorbing shields so the aliens cannot see us.'

'Come, Moins mine, let us go!'

*

'What is that?' hissed Geoffrey to his elder brother, John. He pointed to the shadowed archway of the main entrance. 'A shadow moved ... or something!'

'What? I see nothing.'

His brother was far more experienced and acted nonchalantly. He couldn't let his little brother think he was afraid.

'I smell something too. There's a horrible fishy smell.'

'Must be old Rob's supper. He will eat anything, you know.'

'It doesn't smell like food, though.'

'Well, not to you, maybe. Robert has singular tastes, doesn't he? He –'

John's mouth snapped shut as he clasped his hand desperately over his nose, before keeling over, unconscious.

'John! John!' Geoffrey turned towards his brother as he fell, but had no time to utter anything more as he, too, collapsed on to the cobblestones.

The air next to the two brothers shimmered in three separate sections, appearing something like a heat haze.

'Where are the yellowheads, did you say?' Dollipartonn turned to Broonomarz and quivered his antennae.

'They are through that archway and up the stairs, they are.' Broonomarz indicated the way with his main feeler and drifted smoothly ahead with the other two 'shimmers' following. They floated by several more of the aliens but, luckily, they had no need to disable them physically: their own natural odour did that very effectively. Each one they passed, passed out – in silence, with no upset, no violence and no one noticing what had happened. They were like an invisible, toxic gas.

They glided silently through the stone archway, aliens dropping like flies as they caught a whiff of their special scent. Up the stairs they went – slowly because their tentacles were not used to climbing such structures, but their progress was steady. They neared the top of the staircase and turned the corner, keeping close together.

Two aliens were standing guard outside a wooden entrance. They held lethal-looking, sharp-edged weapons in their hands and wore a metallic covering over their bodies. As the three shimmering shadows approached, one of the guards began to fidget, sniffing suspiciously, his face screwing up in distaste.

'Will! What is that stench? I –'

He collapsed in a heap of clattering metal, followed closely by Will.

The three paused before the door. Broonomarz approached it, producing a shiny, silver-coloured, pistol-shaped implement. He took a deep inhalation of the alien air, then held his breath as he aimed the gadget at the metalwork of the door. The metal began to melt instantly and then disappeared, sucked into the nozzle of the 'atomizer', without damaging the wood of the door at all. The constituent atoms were deposited in the storage compartment of the device, the space between them removed so that the volume was reduced to almost nothing.

Broonomarz pressed his feelers on to the door, with a soft sucking sound. Then he lifted the door out of its frame and moved it quietly to one side.

They glided into the chamber.

Broonomarz gazed down at the two juvenile yellowheads, all his eyes sad. He had discovered that these two juveniles were considered very important. That was why they were so carefully guarded, and he had witnessed several people bending themselves in two in the juveniles' presence, which he thought must be a mark of respect. This should mean they were well fed and had partaken of a diet high in fish. He hoped the guards would not lose too much of their life-time when the two youngsters' disappearance was discovered.

He waved his scent bristles around and they told him he had been correct in his assumption that the high-bred juveniles had eaten much fish. The two were obviously unconscious, because of the proximity of the three Moins and their odour. They would have to mask this once they arrived home with them, so that the experiments could be undertaken while the juvenile aliens were conscious. But for now, the effect of their smell was useful.

They quickly bundled the two into the fabrics they were huddled under and Broonomarz waved his antennae at his two colleagues, who each scooped up a yellowhead, rolled up in their covering, and left the chamber.

He paused outside to replace the door in the frame and took out the atomizer again, reversing the polarity of the contraption so that its disintegrator function became a reintegrator. All the metallic parts flowed out of the nozzle and reformed into the door's metalwork exactly as it had been before their arrival, so that there was no evidence the three Moins had ever been there.

*

'What do you mean they have disappeared? I thought I told you to guard them closely at all times!'

Will and Miles, the two guards, shuffled their feet and glanced at each other.

'We did, Your Grace.' Will bravely met the king's angry gaze. 'Sir Robert Brackenbury made all the arrangements and approved them. We do not know what happened. It seems almost everyone in the Tower was rendered unconscious, but nobody saw anything. The door was still locked when we awoke, but the princes were gone.' He hesitated as the king's eyes narrowed dangerously. 'Nobody was wounded or killed, although we all have a terrible headache. And none of us can abide the smell of fish. It makes us all feel nauseous. Young Geoffrey, the new guard, reckons he smelt fish just before he passed out. Perhaps the Lancastrians have a new weapon?'

'We searched every part of the Tower and they are nowhere to be found.' Miles flushed red as the king turned his frown on him. 'The guards outside the gates of the Tower heard and saw nothing. Nobody arrived or left who cannot be accounted for. The keys were never out of Sir Robert's possession. It is a mystery, Sire. Something fishy is going on – pardon the pun.'

The king paced up and down, his hands balled into fists and a scowl darkening his noble brow.

'How can two royal children, my nephews, disappear from the Tower of London without anyone seeing a thing? What will I tell their mother, Elizabeth? There are already rumours that I have murdered them to safeguard my possession of the throne. If they are not found, I shall never be able to prove my innocence.'

King Richard III pursed his lips and sighed. He had a terrible feeling about this…

About the author

Joanne Larner lives in Rayleigh, Essex, with her husband, John, and two dogs, Jonah, the black lab cross and Hunter, the miniature dachshund. She has worked as an osteopath for more than twenty years, but is interested in many subjects and people. Her latest inspiration is Richard III, who fired her interest when she saw the Channel 4 documentary, *The King in the Car Park*.

Joanne has since read every book she can find on the subject of the last Plantagenet king, but became tired of knowing how they would end, so she finally decided to write her own - a time-travel alternative history called *Richard Liveth Yet*, the 'book she wanted to read'. This then multiplied to a trilogy with the addition of *Richard Liveth Yet (Book II): A Foreign Country* and *Richard Liveth Yet (Book III): Hearts Never Change*. She has also collaborated on two humorous books about Richard with Susan Lamb: *Dickon's Diaries* and *Dickon's Diaries 2* – a madcap mixture of medieval and modern, a cross between the humour of the *Carry On* films and *The Two Ronnies*.

Joanne is currently completing a new novel about Richard, *Distant Echoes*, due out for Christmas 2018.

Website:	https://www.joannelarner.wordpress.com
Amazon:	https://www.amazon.co.uk/Joanne-R-Larner/e/B00XO1IC4S
Facebook:	https://www.facebook.com/JoanneRLarner
	https://www.facebook.com/RichardLivethYet
Twitter:	https://www.twitter.com/JetBlackJo

The Beast of Middleham Moor

Alex Marchant

I shouldn't have done it. Gone that way. It was a stupid thing to do.

A short cut, yes. In the summer. Not the winter.

Not even when it was what Mum called 'early spring', when snowdrops nodded in the shelter of drystone walls and buds of primroses glimmered yellow, nestled among hawthorn roots.

But they'd been at it again. On the bus. The year eights. So old, so superior, they thought themselves.

They'd always done it. To everyone. But now it was worse. Since I'd given them such a fantastic reason.

The best.

Once news of my hospital visits was out.

'Hunchback!'

'Crookback!'

'Spaz!'

I'd had enough. I rang the bell and flung myself to the front of the bus.

The driver was puzzled as the doors folded open.

'This isn't your . . .'

But I was down the step, on to the kerb, didn't glance back.

The doors grated shut, brakes squealed, a glimpse of pale faces pressed against the back window as the bus passed me, and I was alone.

The wind speared the back of my neck. I should have brought my scarf. But Mum in the morning, twittering, put me off.

'Wrap up warm, Jack. Don't forget your scarf. They're forecasting snow.'

I didn't need it, I'd thought then. Five minutes from stop to home. Barely even that.

Don't fuss. Nothing's changed.

But now . . .

I pulled my narrow collar up, hunched my shoulders against the chill, settled the strap of my school bag across my chest.

Looked around.

Not the best place to leave the racket and fug of the school bus.

To one side, grey-wall-bounded fields, speckled white with lamb-heavy sheep. Across the road, only moor.

Heather, bracken, bilberry, stretching up to the horizon. Not purple, golden, blue-pimpled green now. Just every shade of dismal brown beneath the dull grey clouds.

Swelling, bellying clouds.

Snow-heavy clouds.

The footpath sign stabbed upwards, stark against their massing bulk.

The 'short cut'. Across the moor top.

My fingers scrabbled in my pockets. A bus was due in half an hour. If I could find enough cash . . .

Two 10ps and some coppers.

The rest I'd spent on cookies at break time. One for me, one for Joel. He'd taken it, eaten half, then gone back to the others. His friends. Their sniggering had reached my ears before I'd turned away.

A battered old Land-rover grumbled past me as I hesitated on the verge. The first traffic since the bus. It turned into a drive further up the road. Bounced over the ruts towards a grey-stone farmhouse beyond the sheep fields. Ryan and his big brother returning home.

Had he seen me – standing – waiting – for what?

I thrust my hands in my pockets again, crumbs from the cookies digging under my nails.

Looked both ways.

The path was sharp points of icy mud and stones under my smooth-soled school shoes.

Last time I'd been up here, after early autumn rains, water had been standing ankle-deep on the soft peaty soil. Some remained, skatey-hard sheets. I skirted them as I trudged up the hill, and overhanging frozen fronds crunched underfoot.

The narrow way meandered up through the thick plant cover until it met the low grey clouds far ahead. There, I knew, lurked the hollows of the old quarries, overgrown now, but watched over by crouching crags of bare stone. Their blank faces had been cut by men years, maybe centuries, before. Yet no heather or ferns had gained a foothold on their sheer weathered sides.

I paused, looking ahead.

High above, where the moor touched the sky, the clouds became mist, fog even, that danced in the sharpening breeze.

Now was the time to turn back, if I was sensible – to go back to the road, see if my mobile could find a signal, call Mum for a lift if she was at home, or start the long tramp along the tarmac, dodging the speeding cars.

I looked back.

Far off now, in the fields, three figures, bundled in warm camouflage, were slowly urging ewes towards an open gate. Three dogs too, ducking low, darting in black-and-white flashes, circling the sheep.

Ryan and his family, herding them to the shelter of the cluster of barns on their farm.

Before the snow came.

If I were sensible . . .

Ryan. Joel.

'Spaz!'

In a few minutes I was at the top, among the dips and dells and humps left by the ancient quarrymen.

It was hard going. My breath rasped in my throat, the icy wind – whipping up now – knifed inside my nostrils. The mist was twirling closer around me. The once-familiar bump, bump of my school bag had become a dead weight, thumping, pressing – textbook-heavy – against my – back.

My back.

Did it hurt?

No. Not yet.

The pointy textbook corners didn't poke it, didn't hurt. Not through bag canvas, padded jacket. Not yet.

But would they? One day? That weight? Any weight. Any walking? Any climbing?

Before my feet the dark soil, frozen heather, became sandy, gravelly, pebbly. A slope up. A scramble. Almost a climb. Rocks above my head, to the sides, a little stone canyon enclosing a path.

I didn't remember this. Not on my other walks. Had I missed my way in the swirling mist, fog, cloud? It pressed against me now, clammy cold against my face, my hands.

I looked to left, to right.

Only grey, glowering cloud. Brown heather, brown bracken. No other path.

Then came a sharp spike in the breeze, pricking my cheek, the back of my hand. An icy spike. Ice crystals caught on my black padded sleeve.

Snowflakes.

Twirling, whirling snowflakes.

Dancing about my hatless head. Wuthering in my ears. Stinging in my eyes. Chilli-painful on my lips.

I licked them off. They melted on my tongue like a tasteless slush puppy.

I looked back the way I'd come.

Grey snow-shroud cloud, curtaining the whitening heather. A screen of snowflakes hiding the way back. No sign of any path at my feet. Dense bilberries, settling snow. Streaming foggy snow.

There was no way back.

So I had to push on. Up the stony canyon, where flakes were beginning to stick, even where the path was steep. I stumbled. Stones skittered from under my feet, rattling to the bottom. I put out my hands to help my balance, then tipped down on to all fours to scramble up the last slope.

Standing now at the top, beneath my feet the ground was flatter, but a great buffet of wind almost knocked me sideways, snow like hail hammering against me.

I crouched down again. My cheeks were numb now, and my fingers stiffening. As I shoved them in my pockets, I realized for the first time how cold I was. The heat from my anger and shame and the fast walk across the heather was no longer enough. The cold was seeping in all over my body. I started to shiver.

I swung my arms around and thumped them across my chest like they did in films, but all that did was cause flurries in the flying snow.

I looked about me, squinting through the grey-white maelstrom. Only jumbles of rocks and glimpses of scrubby heather beneath their cloaks of snow. No sign now of any path ahead. And in this white wilderness, hemmed in by the blustering fog of snow, I no longer had a clue which way I wanted to go.

Follow the footpath up hill, across the quarried moorland tops. Eventually reach the far side, stand there gazing across wide Wensleydale. Fields beginning far below, edged by grey drystone walls, quarried from these tops. Checkerboard, patchwork, the tourist brochures said.

Follow the path to the road winding through them – from there to the bridge. Across the slow-moving river, then up to Middleham village outskirts, the ruined castle standing proud, on guard, at its highest point. A glance up at the huge flag flapping in the breeze at the top of its tallest tower before opening the front gate and home.

But not today. I had no idea where Middleham was.

Shivers ambushed me again. I had to walk somewhere or I'd be frozen to the spot.

I blundered on forwards, whatever way that was,

my feet sinking into deepening snow drifts. Up to my ankle, then my shin. Then a trip, a stumble forward.

Hands outflung, I landed in the snow.

All wet now, all freezing. The wind still blustering about my ears.

I curled into a ball against the storm, hugging my knees, my back arched above me.

My back.

It didn't hurt, but I could feel it. Arching. Curving. Snowflakes settling on it. Soon it would be all that could be seen of me. Above the snow. If I didn't move.

I lay there motionless, feeling the cold invading me, creeping into my body.

Drowsiness began to steal over me. My thoughts drifted like the snow.

What should I do?

The doctors had said it would only get worse as I got older. Would twist my ribs, squeeze my lungs, perhaps make me struggle for breath. That I should go to hospital to have it fixed, sooner rather than later.

But did I want to?

Perhaps I'd just stay here instead and see what would happen. Now I was starting to feel strangely warm.

Through the raging of the storm, came a different noise.

What was it? The short, sharp bark of a dog? Or a fox?

I moved my head from side to side, trying to shake the sound from my ears.

Why was I lying face down in the snow?

What had happened?

Then I remembered. And knew I must have been dreaming. There was no animal here. Not in this wild whiteness.

And I knew I mustn't stay here – that it was dangerous to be caught in the cold and the snow. That I might die of . . . what was it? Hypo–

I shook my head again to clear it.

Hypo– hypo– thermia – that was it. That was the big word doctors used to mean freezing to death. Why couldn't they just say that?

Like – scoliosis. That was another big word they used. When they could just say 'curve of the spine'.

'Hunchback!'
'Crookback!'
'Spaz!'

I pushed myself to my feet and shook myself like a dog to dislodge the snow. Swaying at the blast of the wind, I stumbled on again. But the wind was so strong, and my feet so frozen and heavy I could barely lift them, and I could still see nothing through the driving snow.

And all around now the darkness was creeping up.

I'd never been on the moortops at night. I'd never been on the moor in snow.

My chest hollowed at the thought, fear gripped me.

How would I get home?

Mum would soon miss me – it was her day off and the school bus would have been and gone by now. But what would she do? She couldn't come and search for me in the snow. She wouldn't know where to start. I had no friends on the bus to let her know. The driver? Perhaps, eventually. But what then?

I'd heard of the Mountain Rescue. They found people. Even round here where there were no mountains. Tourists, walkers, climbers, summer or winter. Anyone who got lost in the dales, fell off crags, injured themselves. Phone 999 they were told.

What about my mobile?

Unslinging my school bag, I squatted down, rummaged in it till my fingers closed on the slim cool shape. I dragged it out. The screen cast a warm glow in the swirling snow.

No signal.
Of course.
Not here, not up on the moortops.

Bloody phone company. And I'd asked Mum for a better phone. Maybe after this . . .

If I got home.

I shoved it back and hunched over the gaping bag, watching snowflakes drift into its dark depths.

Was there anything else in there I could use?

Books mostly. Pens and pencil case. Maths instruments. Remains of my packed lunch. My stomach rumbled, but there were only crusts and an apple core and a biscuit wrapper.

Anything else?

Two conkers left from the autumn in the side zipped pocket, scrunched-up paper, some string. Why?

Then my scrabbling fingers brushed against smooth plastic, and pulled a small object out in triumph.

A lighter!

The one I'd found by the bus stop last week. Translucent red. A spark of colour in the grey-white world, like a fluorescent buoy on a stormy sea.

Straightening up, I shielded my eyes against the waves of wind-driven snow.

Looked all around.

A moment's gap in the icy torrents, a glimpse of – what? A crazy twisted skeleton, stark black against the darkening veil of snow. I stepped forward, saw an ancient, gnarled tree. A gust blew the white curtain across once more.

Shouldering my bag, clutching the lighter, the wind howling around my ears, I battled towards the tree. A hawthorn, clinging to a rocky outcrop at the height of my head. But knobbly roots hung down, a shadowy hollow beyond.

Pushing past the roots, I crawled in. Almost a cave, just big enough for me, bent double. No room for snow to follow. Leaves rustled as I squirmed to get comfortable. A twig cracked.

Sheltered from the worst of the wind, my thoughts cleared. Dry leaves, dry twig?

Scraping a handful or two of leaves into the small space between my shoes, I felt beneath me for the twig. My hand grasped it, broke it into smaller pieces, propped them up on the leaves, wigwam fashion.

My fingers trembling, numb from the cold, I tried the lighter. Once, twice, three times. A flame blossomed. But no leaves or twig caught its fire. Edges smouldered, tiny trickles of smoke were whipped away by wind sneaking in. Even the crumpled paper only charred.

Another try, and another. Still no joy.

The stinging now in my eyes was tears of frustration and fear. Pictures crowded into my mind – rescuers finding a frozen body huddled among tree roots. There was barely room to move, to try to keep warm. I was no longer on the exposed top of the moor, but even here the bitter cold forced its way in.

Soon not only my fingers were numb. From my feet, my bum, my ears and neck, the cold was seeping through me, stealing along my calves and knees, arms and elbows, right into the very heart of me.

Yet as my head filled and my eyelids drooped, warmth grew inside, spread out from my core, washing me on gentle sunlit waves, until . . .

. . . until a sound wormed into my ears. Low and quiet at first, it rose with the wind outside. Until a full-throated primeval howl echoed round my hiding place.

Wolves!

Awake again, alert again, my heart, my mind racing.

Wolves? It couldn't be. There were no wolves in Yorkshire. Surely not anywhere in England.

Yet that howl . . .?

All quiet again, bar the wind's moan.

I hugged my arms around my chest, leaned sideways to peer through the grille of tree roots. Fat snowflakes splattered my face. I wiped them away, blinking to see.

Dark night had closed in. Nothing there but the

still falling snow. But at least no long, grey-whiskered nose or fiery eyes faced me.

But in that moment I remembered – remembered the old tales told around the village.

Of the strange beast that was thought to roam the moors. Not often seen, and then only in darkest shadow; seldom heard, but always on winter's nights, and from far away.

No one agreed on what it was. A gigantic cat or panther escaped from a zoo? A wolf, or werewolf (surely they weren't real)? Or perhaps, some said, the great ghost hound of a long-dead king who had once called Middleham Castle home.

But all were agreed on one thing – it was terrifying.

The hammering of my heart drowned out the tumult outside. I squeezed my eyes tight shut, tried to steady my breathing. Surely surviving a snowstorm was enough for one boy to cope with, without coming face-to-face with the Beastie?

The shock of the howl had sent a surge of fire through me. Now the cold was nipping again. I wriggled my toes and fingers against it, tried to stretch my neck, my back, despite the low roof. But sleepiness began to crawl through me, and with it that weird warming glow.

Perhaps – yes – perhaps I was safe here after all. . .

That was when I heard it.

A voice.

'Boy!'

Outside, not far from my cave.

'Boy?'

More urgent now, louder, above the groaning wind.

'Boy – come. Take my horse.'

Horse? Out there? In this weather?

And who was speaking?

'Hurry, boy! He must be held while I don my mantle.'

A man. The accent was strange – or perhaps just the way of speaking. But –

Was this a rescuer? Had they found me?

But with a horse?

Perhaps that's what they used up here on the moors. In the snow.

The voice spoke again, closer now.

'Come, boy. You must – What? Are you sleeping? In such weather as this? Come, wake up! They say the cold creeps into the mind and brings it dreams of warmth and laughter as at the best of feasts – then steals away your life and soul. Wake up, I say!'

Was that it? What I'd been feeling?

Something wet and very cold struck my ear. I jerked up, hit my head on the roof.

A whimper.

Me or it?

I opened my eyes and saw –

A long, white-whiskered nose next to my face. Brown intelligent eyes.

Heard a bark of laughter from outside.

'Well done, Florette! If he will not wake at my call. . .'

Dog, not wolf.

I breathed again, the air bitter cold still in my nostrils, but tinged with the smell of wet fur.

The dog grinned, pink tongue lolling through sharp white teeth, and backed away. Behind it, a flickering orange glow. A light held aloft. Battered this way and that by snowy gusts, yet enough to show me the scene beyond the trailing hawthorn roots.

A great pale-grey horse, its hooves planted firm in snow reaching up to its fetlocks. Its ears pricked, head tossing against the swirling flakes. Bridle gleaming with silver. Rich embroidered cloth of red and blue beneath its tooled leather saddle.

Before it, the reins loose in one gloved hand, a flaming length of wood in the other, the man who had spoken. He was youngish, younger than my dad. Perhaps no older than Mum's new boyfriend. Thirty, maybe thirty-five. But shorter, slimmer than Callum. And very strangely dressed.

Surely this wasn't Mountain Rescue's normal kit?

All in midnight blue, he wore a padded tunic, or jacket, worked with intricate patterns in silvery thread. Close-fitting leggings of some kind, tucked into sturdy black leather boots. Over the arm that held the reins hung an enormous black fur, long hairs glinting in the flaring light.

An odd hat, perhaps of velvet, upon the man's head, a brooch of blue and red jewels pinned to its side. His hair was brown and long, hanging wet to his shoulders, and framed a pale face. Strong chin, firm nose, blue eyes edged by lines as he peered at me through the veil of snow.

'Well, now you are awake, I see you have greater need of this.'

His voice was gentler now, less abrupt, as he raised the arm with the fur. Then he dropped the reins and plunged the brand, flame uppermost, into the snow.

'Here, boy. I would not have you freeze to death so close to our royal hunting tent. I'm sure with Florette's help we shall find it before long.'

He held out his hand to me. Without thinking, I put out mine to grasp it. Encased in a long gauntlet of deepest blue leather, it hauled me up, out of my hiding place, into the full force of the storm once more.

I gasped as the wind tore away my breath and shooting stars of ice dashed against my face.

That short laugh again. In a moment the huge coal-black fur was swung around my shoulders and my cheeks were nestled in the softness of its hood. The man deftly fastened it somehow, then stood back to view me at arm's length, blinking away the snowflakes from his own face.

'There,' he said, 'now you will live. You may

thank the noble Rus bear that gave up her pelt for you. Would that I had another here, but I see that your clothes are less fit for this winter's day than my own.'

His keen eyes held mine for a moment.

Looked me up and down.

'It is not a page's livery. And I do not recall your face. Are you not one of the household at the castle?'

I shook my head, not sure what he meant, my thoughts still confused.

He seemed to be waiting for something more, as he watched me, the flickering light catching a half-smile playing around his lips.

Thinking of the politeness required at senior school, I added,

'No, sir.'

'You may address me as "Your Grace". Have not your tutors instructed you? Yet, your speech is rough. Perhaps you are a village lad? But now is not the time for talking. We must get you to warmth and meat and drink before you perish. Here, I think perhaps you may ride – maybe our progress will be swifter.'

'Your Grace'? Who was called that? I racked my brain.

Was he a judge? No, that was 'Your Honour' in all the TV programmes. A Member of Parliament? A bishop?

Before I could think any more, he had caught me by the shoulders, propelled me towards his horse, leant down and grabbed my leg, pushing me upwards.

Memories of long-ago riding lessons kicked in, though this was unlike any riding school pony, and I lifted my right leg to edge it across the wide saddle. In a moment I was astride the horse, gazing down at the man's face, shielded from the snow by one hand as he returned my look. I wondered at his strength for so small a man.

'There. No page perhaps, yet you have ridden before. But I will take the reins and guide Storm – you look fit to do no more than cling to him. And he is no doubt a finer mount than you have known before, and more like to throw you if you handle him ill.'

He whistled to the dog, sniffing now around my hiding place, its greyhound shape shaggy with long damp fur. The man rested a hand on its head, breathed a few words I could not catch, then stooped to pluck up the flaming brand. As the hound nosed a path away from the gnarled hawthorn, I wound my stiff fingers into the horse's soaking-wet mane and hoped I could indeed cling on.

The ride seemed to last for ever – the white dog, barely visible as it led the way, head down, tail aquiver, into the onrushing hail of snowflakes; the man striding after, hefting the comforting flare of the torch, the reins again loose in his gauntleted hand; the horse stepping delicately, picking its careful way through the deepening snow; me, leaning more and more towards its proud, curving neck, as I tired, and my back began to ache at the jolt, jolt, jolt of the horse's walk, and I tried to keep out of the pelting snow, and away from the thoughts rushing to haunt me.

Back at the hospital. The surgeon's consulting room. Disney pictures on every wall. Mostly 'Frozen', of course. Ice princesses, snowmen, brave princes. Not really for twelve-year-old boys.

Breaking the news.

Seeing the tears spring in Mum's eyes.

Watching Dad, there for once, his knuckles white, fists clenching.

Looking down.

My chest hollow, heavy weight in my stomach.

What did it all mean?

'You'll be able to lead a normal life, of course. Be able to do most things other kids can. The same, probably, when you're older. But –'

There's always a 'but'.

'But it will get worse. It may become disabling – it's likely to be a severe curve if it's not corrected. You've seen the scans.'

Then the final blow.

'It may even affect your breathing.'

Looking down.

Bitten-down nails. Picking at the strap of my school bag across my knees. We'd come straight from classes.

'But – '

Another 'but'.

'– of course the operation is very successful nowadays. We've come a long way with the treatments even since I've been a doctor. Most people opt for it.'

Most people? Even those as afraid of it as they were of the problem it solved?

'Sooner rather than later is best.'

I was jolted out of my memory – dream? – by a sharp bark. Opening my eyes, I lifted my head a little off the great grey neck.

Groggy, I heard my voice say, 'I heard that before.'

The man turned, a flicker of concern in his eyes.

'What say you, lad?'

'That bark. I heard it when – when I was lying in the snow. Before the wolf howled.'

'Wolf?' His eyes narrowed. 'Nay, lad, there are no wolves in this realm of England. Not since the time of my great-grandsire, Edward.'

'But I heard it.'

'Like as not it was the boarhounds, or the alaunts, baying at the scent. I should not have let them slip after the snow came. And my gentlemen . . .' He was thoughtful a moment, casting his glance around into the snowy murk. 'My gentlemen I have not seen. No matter. That bark was Florette's to tell me she has found something. As here. In time – thanks be to the Saviour – before you slip again into delirium.'

Had I been delirious?

Had I heard boarhounds, or wolves – or a werewolf? The Beastie?

I blinked, dislodging crumbs of ice from my eyelashes.

Saw before us, through the curtain of snowfall, a large shadowy shape. Twice as high as the horse, several times as long, it looked like a huge tent, a marquee perhaps – somehow still standing in the gale, though the sides were billowing and a long red and blue flag flapped furiously on its topmost point. Upon the flag was stitched a white boar with massive tusks amid white roses and the red cross of England.

And I remembered what the man had said earlier.

'So close to our royal hunting tent.'

Royal?

And remembered the local tales of the ghost hound of a long-dead king. A king who had once lived at Middleham castle and whose spirit was thought to haunt the moors.

He halted before the tent, stroked the horse's nose, then offered his hand to me.

I looked down.

The wind blew strands of wet hair across his clear eyes.

His mouth smiled up at me.

His hand . . .

I grasped it. It was solid. As before.

This was no ghost.

Surely.

He helped me to dismount, and bundling the fur about me again, hurried me through overlapping flaps into the tent. He thrust the burning brand into a pile of sticks and logs on the floor before us, then turned to fasten the entrance.

'The horse, Your . . . Your Grace?' I asked, stumbling over the words.

'Storm will be attended to,' he said, turning back to the fire, now crackling, flames throwing dancing shadows on the canvas walls.

Upon those walls were hung shining tapestries of

fantastical beasts – unicorns, gryphons, winged lions – pursued by hunters and huntresses in classical and colourful robes. All around were fine-carved oak chairs and stools with tasselled cushions, iron-bound chests, small tables, set ready with silver jugs and cups and dishes of pastries, fruit, nuts. In a corner a couch or camp-bed, swathed with red fabrics that reflected the firelight, and another huge black bear-skin.

The man guided me to a low stool by the fire and poured deep red liquid into a silver cup he placed on a nearby table. A dish of food followed.

'Eat, drink, warm yourself inside. Then you can remove those wet clothes when . . . when my pages come. They will have a change for you.'

He glanced about him, as though confused for a moment, then went to the red-shrouded bed and sat to take off his boots.

I watched him, taking a sip from the cup. Wine. Rich and smooth, and warming in my throat.

The dog came to lie at my feet, stretching out, her pointed nose towards the fire. I stroked her head. It was solid.

But I thought again about what I had heard.

About that king.

In a history lesson at school, months ago, our first weeks of year seven. Something on the news had prompted a question.

An archaeological dig somewhere. A grave had been found. Maybe a king's grave.

'Who was he, Sir?' a girl asked.

The teacher, surprised by such interest, said, 'If it is him – and they're not sure until they do some scientific tests – it's King Richard the Third. He died more than five hundred years ago, but, you probably know, for much of his life he lived not far from here, in Middleham.'

'Why's he so interesting, Sir?'

'Apart from the local angle? Well, he was king for only two years. Some say he's only interesting because

William Shakespeare wrote a play about him.'

'Oh, Shakespeare.'

'Bor-ring.'

'But why, Sir?' persisted the girl.

'We don't actually know that much about his reign, though we know that he passed good laws and had them written in English, not French, for the first time, so everyone could understand them. But a hundred years later Shakespeare painted him as the blackest villain possible – a monster really. Who committed the worst of crimes. But some people say that was just lies, told to please Queen Elizabeth the First, whose grandfather stole the throne from him.'

'What crimes, Sir?'

'What sort of monster?'

'What did he do?'

'Well, Shakespeare said he was born with a hunchback, and a withered arm, and that he murdered his way to stealing the throne, including killing his own wife and his two little nephews.'

'His little nephews, Sir? Did he eat them too?'

The girl next to me went pale at that so-innocent question, but there were sniggers at the back of the class.

The teacher very calmly said, 'No, Ryan,' he already knew his name, 'even Shakespeare didn't claim that. We don't really know whether they were murdered at all – they just seemed to disappear from the Tower of London. King Richard was killed in battle against Henry Tudor, who then claimed the throne. But it's said that Henry was always afraid the two boys would come back again – because they had a better claim to be king than he did – and he didn't know for sure whether they were dead or alive, despite all the later talk of murder.'

And that had been all. On with the Tudors – so much more to grab twelve-year-olds' attention. All those wives, beheadings, burnings at the stake, the Armada, Shakespeare himself. One king of only two years, who might or might not have murdered people, was never going to be so interesting – even if he was a local boy.

But who would be called 'Your Grace'? Not a king, surely. He would be 'Your Majesty', wouldn't he?

The man had now shrugged off his thick outer jacket, which hung dripping from a chair back. He stood for a moment in a pale, thin shirt, rubbing one shoulder, his glance flicking to every corner of the dry, warm tent. Then a smile tugged at a corner of his mouth and he said to me,

'It seems not just my gentlemen, but pages and squires also are lost in this wild night. My back is sore from riding so long today. Lad, will you do me a small service?'

From his gesture, I saw what he wanted, and leaving the bear-skin cloak behind, I hurried to help. I gripped the hem of his long, soft shirt and hauled it upwards. But it became caught around his shoulders. As I struggled to free it, from the depths of the fabric I heard again his short bark of a laugh.

'Lost also, it seems, is a king with no attendants about him.'

At last I managed to ease the shirt up and over his head. I pulled it away from him, stunned by what I'd heard.

Who was he? A madman, with delusions of grandeur? But with a horse, a hound, a tent hung with beautiful tapestries . . . ?

Or –?

As I dropped the damp shirt next to the jacket, he reached across to fetch a dry one from a chest. And I saw his back, bare in the warm fire-glow – and the deep shadows cast by the curve in his spine, dancing in the flickering light of the flames.

I looked, and could not tear my eyes away.

Until he slipped the clean, dry shirt over his head, and the fabric fell like a curtain over the scene.

I had seen that sight before. In the hospital.

The surgeon passing Mum, Dad, me, photos. Of

other people's backs. White, black, brown, boys, girls, older than me, none perhaps younger.

What my back would look like in a year, two years, five, ten.

If I didn't have the operation.

My voice stuttered out without permission.

'But – but you can ride!'

He swung round, still fastening the neck of his shirt, a questioning frown upon his face.

'Ride? Aye, lad, of course. Why –?'

Then his eyes cleared and the ghost of a smile returned.

'My back? Aye, it does not stop me riding – though it grows more painful year by year. And my armour seems to weigh more heavily every season. But I bear it, by God's mercy. A king must do no less. It has never stopped me riding into battle or dispensing justice.'

And it was not a hunchback.

He drew a dark red jacket from the same chest and pulled it on, thanking me as I eased the second sleeve over his arm and shoulder. Then waved me to another chest across the tent.

'As it seems we must fend for ourselves tonight, find such dry clothes for yourself as you may in there. Then return to the fire if you will. We have no minstrels or mummers to entertain us here. Perhaps we should gather round the flames and tell ghost stories as we hear the villagers do on long winter's nights.'

The faint smile remained.

Did he know?

Then a thought struck me.

If he were a ghost . . . was I?

A cold wet muzzle pushed against my hand. The hound, Florette. Her trusting brown eyes stared up at me.

I patted the coarse fur of her head before going to the second chest to see what I could find.

In a few minutes, my wet school uniform was draped across various chairs and I had dressed again in leggings, shirt and tunic – halved in deep red and blue – with soft shoes upon my feet.

He sat now by the fire, gazing into its depths, nursing a silver cup in both hands. Florette lay across his feet, muzzle upon her outstretched forepaws.

The dish of food lay untouched at his elbow. I didn't feel like eating either. What if I couldn't feel it, taste it?

Yet I remembered the comforting warmth of the wine.

I picked up a small, bright-skinned orange before returning to my seat.

I sat across the dancing flames from him, sitting straight and tall on the low stool as I watched him. Somehow I found my voice again.

'Does it still hurt – Your Grace?'

He looked up at me. The firelight glittered in the depths of his eyes.

'Not so much now, I thank you. Now, did you ever hear tell of the great wild ghostly beast that men say roams far and wide across these, our windswept, snow-clad moors? On winter's nights, when good folk are safe around their firesides, and they hear the howl of the wind, or is it that of the beast . . .?'

Long tales and many he knew, and told me that night, that chilled me to the bone and made me laugh out loud by turns. I thought of the minstrels who had told them to him and the people of his household, and the mummers who had acted them out, and as time passed, and the wine warmed, and his voice quietened, and the flames died, I must have slipped at last into sleep.

*

They found me just after first light. It wasn't a large area of moor to search, they said. The Mountain Rescue, in their high-viz outdoor gear, with their two-way radios and their Land-rovers.

I was curled up next to a strange white dog in a hollow at the foot of an old gnarled hawthorn. Among the dips and dells and humps left by ancient quarrymen on our windswept, snow-clad moor.

They took me straight to hospital to check me for hypothermia, frostbite, pneumonia, all the big words they could think of. They thought I was delirious, with my tales of the Beastie and the long-dead king.

Perhaps I was.

Mum and Dad were both there waiting for me. The Rescuers had called to let them know I'd been found. Callum would come to see me later, said Mum. So would Sue, said Dad. When I'd been given the all clear.

They hugged me as they always used to. Fully and properly, as if there were no twist, no curve, lurking beneath my clothes.

My clothes. My dry school uniform, just a little wet and frosty at the edges.

The dog had run off, the Rescuers said. It hadn't had a collar, they said. They couldn't catch it.

Must have belonged to one of the farms scattered across the moor.

Lucky it had been there. That it had been enough to keep me warm and save my life during the freezing cold, stormy night.

Dad drove us both home. I sat in silence in the back as they talked – as always – about the divorce. Lawyers, fees, court dates, custody.

We drove through the newly gritted marketplace, past the ancient stone cross with its cap of white, the broken tower of the castle rising high above the snowy roofs, pulled up at the wooden gate. I let myself in at the front door. They finished their conversation outside, despite the freezing morning.

When Mum came in, I was sitting with her laptop on my knees. I had already googled 'King Richard the Third'. To my surprise, not Wikipedia, but something else came up first.

A news broadcast.

Men and women sitting in a line behind desks, in front of hoardings full of logos. Smiles on their faces. People with cameras crouching in front of them.

A close-up of a dark-haired woman.

Her name on the caption.

Dr King.

Was that why Google had directed me to this?

Before I could click away, her words caught my ears, before cheers and clapping began.

'. . . beyond all reasonable doubt, we have found King Richard the Third.'

Behind her now, I saw a large projection of a skeleton in a grave. The curve in its back was clear to see. Next came a photo of a man's back. The word 'reconstruction' beneath it.

Another photo.

That curve.

Pale skin, not cast in shadows by flickering firelight.

A blonde woman now, a half-smile upon her face. Asked questions, answering them.

I could hardly concentrate, my mind was so full of strange thoughts.

But two sentences stood out.

'We now know King Richard was not a hunchback, despite what Shakespeare wrote. We know now instead that he had scoliosis, a lateral curvature of the spine, and though he would probably have been in a great deal of pain, it would not have prevented him riding and fighting, and being the brave warrior king that the real history has always told us.'

'Jack, love?'

Mum stood in the doorway, an opened letter in her hand. On it, the logo of the hospital we'd just left.

'The date for the operation has come. I know we've already discussed it, and I know you weren't keen, but do you think we could talk about it again? I know it'll mean you'll have to be very brave.'

I looked up at her and smiled.

'It's OK, Mum. I've thought about it some more. You can tell Dr Lovell I think I'll do it.'

Relief washed across her face.

Would she let me do what I wanted to now?

'Could I have some money to go to the castle, please?'

'The castle? I'm not sure it's open. Why?'

I couldn't explain. Just handed her the laptop where the news broadcast was still talking about King Richard.

She gave me a fiver from her purse, wrapped me in my thickest coat – and scarf and hat – and waved me off at the door.

A minute or two and I'd trudged across the marketplace and was winding up the snowy lane to the main gate.

The huge grey-stone gatehouse loomed above me as I crossed the icy bridge over the moat. The modern wooden gate was closed, but as I walked up, a flash of white passed me and slipped easily between the bars.

Beyond, a woman flung herself to her knees, despite the thick snow, and caught it in a hug.

'At last,' I heard her gasp.

The flash was a shaggy, white, long-nosed dog.

The woman saw me watching and straightened up.

'Hello. Can I help you? I'm afraid we're not open yet. But I'm the new manager here.'

'Here?' I said. 'At King Richard's castle?'

'That's right. Do you know its history then?'

She must have thought me daft, or mad, standing there, knee-deep in snow, staring past her at the dog. But she saw where I was looking and said simply,

'That's my dog. She went missing last night in the snow as I was locking up here. I was worried sick. She's only just come back. Do you like her? Her name's –'

'Florette.'

She looked at me strangely for a moment, then gave a short laugh.

'Yes, it is. How did you know?'

Beyond her, on the tallest snow-capped tower, flapped a great banner, red, blue, with a boar stitched in white.

About the author

Alex Marchant was born and raised in the rolling Surrey downs, but, following stints as an archaeologist and in publishing in London and Gloucester, now lives surrounded by moors in King Richard III's northern heartland, not far from his beloved York and Middleham.

A Ricardian and writer since a teenager, Alex's first novel, *Time out of Time* (due out 2019), won the 2012 Chapter One Children's Book Award, but was then put on the backburner in 2013 at the announcement of the rediscovery of King Richard's grave in a car park in Leicester. Discovering that there were no books for children telling the story of the real Richard III, Alex was inspired to write them, and so *The Order of the White Boar* and its sequel *The King's Man* were born. Together they tell King Richard's story through the eyes of a young page who enters his service in the summer of 1482, and have been called 'a wonderful work of historical fiction for both children and adults' by the *Bulletin* of the Richard III Society and 'exciting, appealing and refreshing' by the publication of Richard III's Loyal Supporters (www.r3loyalsupporters.com).

Website:	https://alexmarchantblog.wordpress.com
Amazon:	https://www.amazon.co.uk/Alex-Marchant/e/B075JJKX8W/
Facebook:	https://www.facebook.com/AlexMarchantAuthor/
Twitter:	https://twitter.com/AlexMarchant84
GoodReads:	https://www.goodreads.com/author/show/17175168.Alex_Marchant

Joanna Dreams

Máire Martello

Joanna dreams. In mist, she dreams. She dreams of a bright object that fades into mist. When she wakes, like many people who dream, she remembers nothing.

She is pressed to marry by her brother, King John of Portugal, a son of the English House of Lancaster. She is the Infanta Joanna and many rulers seek her hand. They wish to make strong alliances with Albion – that great nation of trade and travel. She rejects them all; she wishes only to marry Christ. Brought before her brother and his court, she is insulted and bullied into choosing a suitor. King John reminds her of her age and mocks her long sad face which draws no man's interest. In her darkened room, she weeps and prays that God will deliver her to the Dominican Sisters in Aveiro.

As she twists and turns, hot under her coverlet, she falls into troubled slumber. Mist rises and through it she sees an image that shines as bright as Canis Major, the Dog Star. She reaches out for this precious object, but as she does, it again disappears before her eyes. She wakes, but unlike other times, she remembers. She is startled, but not unhappy at her dream.

Her brother presses her again: he would like her to marry King Charles of France. But he is a child of fifteen and she turns away in horror. She is thirty-three years old.

That evening the dream becomes as sharp as it never was before. It's as if she was looking through a new invention called the *camera obscura*. The bright shining object comes close and appears to be polished armour. It is the kind of armour that might be worn by a knight. She looks desperately for a face, but all she sees is a slender white hand extending a white rose – for her? She's unsure but reaches for it all the same. It falls into the mist.

Still the negotiations go on with King Charles of France. He is said to be a pleasant boy, but Joanna only wants to be reunited with Christ. This boy-king, she knows, will bring her despair. But her dark and powerful brother frightens her so that she appears to agree to the marriage.

So Joanna dreams. And in this dream, she sees the entire figure of the knight. He holds out another white rose to her. He is more beautiful than any man she has ever seen – as if he has walked out of the sun. He is tall with soft blue eyes and tumbling blond hair and the sweetest curve upon his tender lips.

Who is he? she wonders. What hope does he bring her? He seems to be encouraging her, but she cannot make out his words – she cannot hear in her dreams.

He draws a veil aside and she sees a young prince on a wide unknown plain. He is quite different from the golden knight. He is lean and dark-haired and he sits proudly on a tall white stallion. He wears a quilted tabard over his armour. The tabard is sewn with the flag of St George. Around the knight's head is a fiery circlet of gold. He has a serious, quiet face with intelligent grey eyes. She would even say a pious face. He turns his head and beckons to her. Joanna runs to meet this intriguing prince, forgetting all thoughts of duties to the realm or the convent.

When she awakes, she pounds her pillow and cries tears of frustration that she cannot speak to the soldier prince. She no longer thinks of her marriage to Christ. Instead, she dwells on the young man on the tall white horse. She sinks to her knees and prays that God forgives her failing vocation.

Great wars are coming to England. Joanna hears this at a distance. Her brother wants to build an alliance with Yorkist England and Portugal. He believes the two houses of Lancaster and York can be reunited and thus end the terrible War of the Roses. These wars have devastated England and created havoc on the continent.

'Dear Joanna,' says her brother, 'I have a new offer for your hand in marriage. He has been a widower for a year and he is quite young. He is close to your age – thirty-two. He has been kind enough to send a small portrait of himself. Would you care to look at it?'

Joanna, still dream-walking towards her soldier prince, is not inclined to look. Nonetheless, she slips it out of its white silk cloth curiously embroidered with a tusked boar. The small portrait shows quite a nice face – calm grey eyes, straight lips and high cheekbones. His hair is dark and long. The only hint that he is a man of substance is the heavy gold collar of office he wears upon his shoulders. His expression is so serious, so pious—

Her heart beats faster.

'Who is this, Brother?'

'It is Richard, King of England. He wishes to marry you.'

'Is he a soldier?'

'One of England's greatest. It has been the sum total of his career until he assumed the throne of England.'

'What is he like, Brother?'

The king sighs. He is bemused by his sister's many foolish questions about her various suitors.

'He is a good king and a widower without issue. Do you like the portrait?'

'He is not unfamiliar.' She smiles secretly.

Seeing for once that she is not obdurate, he leans down and kisses her upon her high white forehead. She returns to her room admiring the portrait.

No knight-angel visits her that night. She wakes disappointed but not unhappy. She attends her brother the king and tells him she agrees to marry Richard. He is overjoyed and swings her up in his arms and dances with her about the gallery. The entire court is overjoyed.

Still a virtuous woman, she continues to pray to the Virgin Mary and partake of Holy Communion.

Eventually, a silky diplomat, Sir Edward Brampton, arrives from London and begins negotiations for the marriage. After several days of signing contracts, King John asks his sister to pray and meditate on this marriage. She humbly agrees, suppressing her happiness lest he be wary and mock her unaccustomed gaiety.

That night, Joanna dreams.

He appears before her. He opens his brightly coloured tabard and many white roses tumble towards her. She laughs and grabs at them, and he smiles and laughs in return. He mounts his beautiful horse, turns once to take her into his mind's eye and rides away. She stumbles towards him awkwardly, but he is lost in mist. When she wakes, she knows she'll never be as happy as she is this day.

August of 1485 arrives and King Richard, it is reported, is heading to a place called Redmore Plain to fight a battle against an upstart named Henry. The court of Portugal laughs at such a fool. Joanna does not laugh, but retreats to the cold dark stone chapel in the palace to say the rosary for his safety.

Again, Joanna dreams. The mist arises and she hears the sound of distant drums. Her knight-angel returns and swiftly draws back the veil to reveal her soldier prince, King Richard. But he is no longer upon his great steed. He is on his knees before her. Again, he opens his tabard to present her with white roses and she rushes towards him. But the flowers are not white. What tumbles out are red roses, but as they continue to fall in multitudes, she realizes that they have turned to blood – rivers of blood. She tries to staunch his wounds with her hands. She wipes away the bloodied hair from his face. The angel draws the veil and mouths words that she can barely hear.

'Your Richard is gone from the living.'

Joanna wakes screaming. To the horror of her ladies-in-waiting, she is covered in blood. Her hands are red with it as are her face and nightdress. A doctor is summoned, but they cannot find any wounds upon her body. All they can find are white roses scattered on the bed; but the thorns could not draw so much blood. The court is in an uproar; even an astrologer is brought in to solve the mystery. Joanna fights them off tigerishly, refusing to change out of her soiled gown with its precious blood.

King John finally prevails. She is helped into fresh clothes and put to bed with magical draughts that will make her sleep.

But like many people who dream, she dreams of nothing.

About the author

Máire Martello is a playwright currently living in Manhattan.

14th April 1471 – Blooding

Matthew Lewis

An excerpt from *Loyalty*

Mist clung to the glistening, dewy hilltops, refusing the warm draw of the sun that stood proudly at the rim of the clear spring sky. Though the sun was not shaded, a chill still cut through the air and tickled at the back of the neck of a rider who sat alone, looking almost like a ghost atop a dark demonic horse in the lingering haze. His mount stomped its front hoof in the damp grass with a dull thud, spraying moisture fully half the way up its own leg as the rider tugged at its reins to contain the horse's excitement. Clearly the beast knew what was to come, even if its rider could only wish that he did.

'How does it look, brother?'

The voice made the man jump in his saddle, but the alarm was momentary as he well knew the sound of it.

'Cold, wet and foggy, sire.' The reply was somewhat solemn and brought a deep frown to the brow of King Edward.

'You are nervous, Richard.' It sounded more a command than an enquiry.

Richard, Duke of Gloucester, shot a hard gaze over his shoulder at his brother, whose own horse was moving alongside him, and replied shortly,

'No, sire. I have come here to do my duty this day, to my country, to my king and to my brother.' His gaze turned into the haze before them. 'Today, here at Barnet, you will reclaim your throne and your exile will end.' Richard kept his tone deep, thinking this to be the best way to mask the dread he truly felt in his very core.

'Our exile, Richard, shall end. It was ours together

and we shall return to London together in triumph.'

Edward thought for a moment. He had forgotten that his brother was only eighteen years of age and that this was to be his first taste of the mud of a battlefield.

'Do not think,' he continued in a softened tone, 'that your loyalty has gone unnoticed these long months. Your support has been the bedrock upon which I have built my return, and where our brother's blood has fuelled his own ambition, yours has thickened your loyalty.'

Perhaps Edward over-stated the measure of his brother's importance, but then perhaps not. Either way, he felt it would serve to stiffen Richard's resolve.

'Thank you, sire,' Richard replied, his eyes darting back to his brother. 'But I need no thanks for doing right, Edward. I would serve a thousand exiles with you and not falter.'

He smiled for the first time since his brother had startled him, allowing only a faint upturning of his thin lips. His slender nose sniffed at the cold air. He looked little like his brother, who was tall and broad as Richard was slender and of a more normal height.

'By God, no!' Edward roared loudly. 'I have had enough exile to last me a hundred lifetimes!'

Rearing his horse, he laughed heartily and called down the hill behind him to where the mist concealed ranks of soldiers who stood like figurines on a child's playroom floor.

'Draw up the lines!' he bellowed.

His command was echoed by a dozen lesser voices and a great clamour grew as each part of the assembled mass ground into motion, lurching like a wheel stiffened by a lack of use, until it eventually moved smoothly up the hill to draw up around its leader.

'Do not ignore your fear, Richard,' Edward spoke softly again as his army obeyed his words.

'I am not afraid, my king,' Richard snapped defensively.

He did not want his brother to know the dread that

gnawed on his stomach like some disease-ridden rat on an old rope. More than anything else he craved his brother's respect as a man and as a soldier. Edward was ten years his elder, and Richard had always been aware of his stature, as king and as a man who stood a full foot taller than himself; though Richard was not particularly short, he had long since given up hope of matching his brother. He was lithe while his brother was broad and imposing. Edward was proven in battle and commanded respect, and Richard wanted desperately to be like the king he served.

'If you are not afraid, then you are a fool, brother.' Edward was blunt and Richard smarted at the jibe, though that had not been the effect that his brother had desired. The young man felt himself blush, and thanked the heavens for the cool air that hid the worst of it. He bit his lip hard in anger at the apparent disapproval of his brother and at his own inability to control his reaction. Unable to answer, he simply stared into his brother's eyes, but was surprised to see only a look of concern rather than ridicule within them.

'Your fear is your own spirit guarding you against harm. Ignore it, and you lose its protection. Listen to it and it will keep you safe. God has no desire to see any of us die, and so he gave us fear to protect us.'

The brothers looked at each other for a long moment, not as a king to his noble subject, but as men bound by a love that transcends a feudal relationship. Almost as one, they then nodded to each other as if an agreement had been reached in the silence.

'God be with you, Richard.'

The king turned his horse to assume his position at the head of this army that he hoped would help him to begin the reclaiming of his throne.

'And may He speed you to your rightful victory, sire.'

Watching his brother disappearing into the lingering fog to his left, Richard placed a hand upon the pommel of his sword, swallowed hard and asked God to deliver him safely from this field.

It seemed an age that the wall of men and metal stood unmoving upon the hill. The only sound was the stamping of the hooves of excited horses as they sensed the mounting tension. Somewhere ahead in the mist could be heard the ghostly clinking and thudding that signified the enemy's assembly not too far in front.

Richard looked down from his mount on to the field where this battle would take place at any moment. He could not see even the grass as the fog thickened but sank low. Perhaps it lingered to see the outcome of this day. The horse fidgeted beneath him, puffing great plumes of hot breath that mingled with the surrounding cloak of mist and were gone. Whatever was to happen on this field today, Richard reflected that God must not want to see it. That worried him. Fear began to rise from his stomach and he felt it lodging in his throat as if it tried to escape and shout to the world that Richard of Gloucester was afraid for his life. He closed his lips tightly to prevent this release, looking around him at his retinue. He wondered what they all felt now. He also wondered whether they knew how he felt, whether his face betrayed the fears of his mind. Now, he felt physically sick as silence descended for a brief moment on both sides of the field.

'Charge!'

The voice of King Edward IV broke through the fog like a rolling thunder through a quiet night sky. The sound of a thousand men running down the hill, noisily drawing swords, rang in Richard's ears as he momentarily forgot himself before digging his heels sharply into the sides of his mount. As the horse gathered speed to a gallop down the gentle slope of the hillside, the mêlée that awaited became unavoidable. The horse would carry him to the very thick of it, and Richard found that this notion calmed the acid in his throat a little. He drew his sword and spurred the horse on faster to meet the enemy.

Suddenly, everything around the young man

seemed to slow down, like some strange theatre piece. The clamour about him was drowned out by the pounding of his own heart like a beating drum and the sound of blood rushing in a raging torrent through his head. Then, in a blink of his wind-filled eyes, the din returned, enhanced by the now clearly approaching Lancastrian line.

Richard squinted into the thinning mist as wraith-like warriors began to emerge, ethereal, as if floating towards him. Raising his sword to shoulder height, the rider allowed a smile to trace itself across his lips at the thought of all those shadows that had provided the only test of his swordsmanship to date. As these shadows began to form solid shapes Richard gritted his teeth hard and swung his sword downwards. The two lines met like a mighty wave crashing into the immovable cliffs of Dover and Richard's arm jarred painfully. Looking down, he saw an armoured figure falling backwards, livery and a chainmail vest cleaved open from naval to chest and framed in bright red blood which reached out and licked at his forearm. Finally, Richard was tasting the nervous excitement of battle. And it felt good.

Raising his sword again, he spied his next target and again his weapon deftly met its mark with a reassuring thud and another jar that reached his shoulder. Either side of him, Richard heard the sound of steel upon steel and the howls of those who failed to avoid an oncoming weapon.

Unbeknownst to either commander, the mist had caused the opposing lines to form up off centre. While the Yorkist right found scant resistance, the left flank was routed. The battle pivoted uneasily around the clatter and clamour of the fierce mêlée at its centre. As the Lancastrian right regrouped, aiming to wheel left to engage the Yorkist centre, the fog all but blinded their charge until they were upon their target. Only then did they spy the livery of those they raised their swords against – and saw it matched their own.

For a moment an eerie silence reigned as this front line of the Lancastrian right realized who stood before them – the Lancastrian centre being charged by its own right flank. The second line of men, unable to see, failed to halt their charge. They pushed through their own line with a blood-curdling scream, designed to inspire fear within the enemy. Instead it caused an immediate cry of treason from the Lancastrian ranks.

Richard, meanwhile, had ploughed a furrow through the Lancastrian lines, leaving behind him a dozen bloodied corpses. His retinue were struggling to keep up and several had fallen. Hearing the cries of betrayal from his left, Richard halted and swung his horse around, unsure what he should do. Uncertain even if the cries of treason came from within the Yorkist ranks or those of the enemy, he was suddenly lost, his confidence evaporating with the mist and deserting him.

The Lancastrian army loyal to King Henry began to peel away from the engagement from right to left and the Yorkist lines gave chase for a short while, with a few straggling Lancastrians being picked off as the retreat became complete. Richard sat astride his mount in the midst of the corpses and those struggling noisily to cling on to their lives, his sword gripped so tightly in his right hand that his knuckles were whitened and he could no longer feel his fingers. He gazed, mesmerized, at the sight of what had just occurred, as a passer-by may stumble upon the scene of a roadside ambush and stare at the murdered corpses with sorrow for their suffering and disgust for those who would perpetrate such a dire act. He felt strangely detached from what surrounded him in spite of his own involvement in the scene.

Looking down, he could see the faces of those his own hand had slain. Previously they had been featureless targets, but now he could see their vacant eyes peering into the clouding skies as if for a last glimpse of the spirit that had already vacated their mortal bodies. Closing his eyes, Richard tried to force down the guilt that he already felt rising in his stomach. Surely, this was not how a soldier was supposed to feel upon the field of victory. His brother must not feel this weakness, so neither would he. With his eyes shut tightly he drew upon the excitement that he had felt in the raw, searing heat of the battle and resolved to keep that as a cork to contain all the other feelings. Opening his eyes, Richard turned his horse and began to canter back along the distance that he had charged towards the encampment. He never once looked down again as he retreated to the moral sanctuary of his tent.

Pushing aside the canvas at the entrance, the young duke released the breath that pounded in his chest and, without willing his hand to do so, he released the grip that he had maintained on his red, stained weapon. It clattered as it hit the ground. Immediately, he plunged his hands into the bowl of icy water that stood beside the entrance, not noticing the cold biting his fingers. He stood motionless and watched, with a frown playing across his forehead, as thin tendrils of deep scarlet spread from his hands across the surface of the water as though taking it over. It made him feel sick. Quickly, before all the clear water was lost, he cupped his hands and threw handfuls of the water into his face to remove the grime of battle, and perhaps the guilt he was feeling too. He shivered at the cold. A strange trembling gripped at his limbs. As he moved to the large oak chair to the left of the tent, he stripped away the armour that was flecked with an awful mixture of mud and blood, along with the clothes beneath it which bore splatters of both too, and collapsed into the seat, instinctively reaching to the nearby table for the leather-bound prayer book that was his almost constant companion. In spite of his will to feel no need for it, he opened the book and read for more than two hours, alone.

When he emerged, Richard squinted as he pushed the heavy fabric of his tent door. The midday sun was warm on his cheeks as he strolled through the lush green grass to the king's opulent red and blue marquee. Stepping inside, the smell of roasting meat confronted him like another curtain to be pushed through. The air was thick and hung heavy in his nostrils and his mouth began to water as he tasted the sweet scent drawn over his taste buds. The noise died down as those gathered around the king realized that the duke had entered. Richard was becoming aware of a strange sensation in his legs as he stood still, when his brother called from the table with a natural authority that Richard had always felt truly befitted a king.

'Ah, brother!' Richard looked at the king and an uneasy smile passed fleetingly across his lips. 'We began to fear that you had disappeared in the mist of this morning.'

Richard winced as the flattering, raucous laughs of the gathered lords at the king's table bellowed around the tent. About a dozen men, all of whom had now forgone their armour in favour of the lavish finery of court clothing, sat at a long table erected in the king's tent and were devouring several roasted boars.

'Come and sit at my side, Richard.' Edward gestured grandiosely to the empty place setting at his right side. The young man shifted uncomfortably on his soles, brushed his damp palms down his thighs and strode around the table to the seat set by for him. The honour of the position saved for him was in no way lost on the duke, but he did not share his brother's taste for the more tangible trappings of power. Fawning old men and overconfident young lords irritated Richard. They served no real purpose other than to inflate the ego of whosoever could provide them with the warmest shelter today. At the first sign of a chill, they immediately sought warmer climates. Always sure not to leave the old shelter before the new was secured and proven safe.

'The hounds offer you better loyalty than these men,' Richard thought as he sat down, glancing at his brother's three large hunting hounds. 'And they have better table manners too.' A smile brushed his lips as he eyed the carnage along the table and the surrounding floor.

Richard suddenly became aware that his brother was staring at him, and almost jumped, as though the king might have read his thoughts and disapproved. He shifted under his brother's heavy gaze. Even sitting, Edward dwarfed Richard's lithe young frame. Richard's abiding childhood memory of his brother had always been of his size and strength. He was convinced that Edward's stature alone was demonstration of his credentials as ruler of England. Disappointed to have more resembled their father, Richard knew he would never lose his respect for and dread fear of his brother and king.

'Sire?' he questioned his brother's intense stare softly. As much respect as he had for his king, his brother had never made him feel anything other than a beloved younger sibling. Perhaps, Richard always considered, the ten-year gap between them increased the protective, nurturing feeling that he hoped his brother felt for him.

'I was getting worried about you, Richard.' Edward spoke in a soft tone that mirrored his brother's, but which also prevented the others around the table from hearing. 'Where did you get to?' he queried, his voice full of concern. Edward was fully aware that this had been Richard's first taste of battle and he well remembered the floods of opposing emotions that the experience could release.

'I needed a little time alone, Your Grace.' Richard tried not to sound feeble, but his head sank as he spoke, aware that his admission could easily be construed as weakness. There was a prolonged pause. Even in the clamour of the feasting, it felt to Richard like a hollow silence.

'You must be feeling raw.' Edward's tone had not changed. The concern was a surprise to Richard. A pleasant one, though.

Edward saw the frown fold itself into his brother's brow. He studied the fresh, young face before him. At eighteen, Richard was his most trusted subject, beyond even Lord Hastings at his other side. This brother was one of the few men whose loyalty he had never yet had cause to question. They had shared two long, harsh periods of exile and Richard had never shown any sign of wanting to be anywhere but at Edward's side. He had, by virtue of his birth, ascended to high office before the rebellion they now sought to quell, but this had been his first real chance to prove himself as a man. Edward had found Richard something of an enigma. Difficult to get close to, yet fiercely loyal to his family. When their cousin the Earl of Warwick had risen in rebellion the previous year, it was Richard who the king had most keenly awaited to declare his hand, and when Richard had not hesitated to support him, Edward had felt a deep guilt for doubting his brother. He comforted himself that blind faith was not a luxury that he could afford. Warwick had, after all, recruited their other brother, George, Duke of Clarence to his cause. Richard, however, had not hesitated to board the ship with Edward at King's Lynn on that wet 2nd October last year. The date of their enforced flight had not been lost on Edward. As King of England, he had hoped to reward his brother with a far more enjoyable day to celebrate his eighteenth birthday. Richard had never even mentioned it.

'Battle,' Edward leaned deliberately into his brother, 'affects all men in different ways. I have seen men who boast of their prowess piss themselves as a charging enemy approaches.'

Edward leaned forward and raised his tankard to a broad, middle-aged man further along the table who Richard vaguely recognized. The man ceased his rolling laughter to raise his own goblet in the king's direction with a nod. Edward turned back to Richard with a cheeky smirk on his face. Clearly, that was one of the men he spoke of. Richard smiled too.

'I have also seen the very opposite,' Edward continued, suddenly serious, 'and I saw it in you today, Richard.' Edward smiled broadly again. 'The quietest, most reserved man may become a wild animal on the battlefield. War can turn a man inside out and he may even surprise himself.'

Richard nodded, unsure how else to respond. Edward sat back into his chair and raised his voice now to address all around.

'Today, we rise again, brother.' The king beamed and all around were instantly silenced, focused upon him.

'Today is Easter Sunday, sire.' Richard still spoke softly and only to his brother.

'True.' Edward's voice boomed through the silence of the tent now. He rose from his chair to his full height. A magnificent sight that had served Edward well. He clumsily grabbed a goblet of wine from the table. 'To God, and His England!' he called and his salute was echoed by all of the gathered lords.

Richard mouthed the words with a silent reverence and looked up to see the towering figure of the king looking directly into his eyes.

'To our risen Saviour,' Edward toasted more soberly.

The toast was again echoed, also somewhat soberly.

Richard smiled at his brother, knowing that this toast had been made for his benefit. He noted, though, that the religious sentiment raised less passion amongst those gathered than the self-praising of patriotism. Richard already had a reputation as a pious man, which he wanted to be proud of, but he knew that to feel so would be considered a sin. He knew from recent history, though, that the temporal world required more from a man of his position than just pious devotion. That alone was what had led his own family to imprison King Henry within the Tower. Richard fully appreciated that a more rounded worldview was necessary to retain power. Today, he had taken his first step towards this position.

A further hour passed with little eating and much drinking before many of the lords departed with varying degrees of drunken swaying, and only a few remained snoring loudly where they had slumped at the table.

'Richard.' Edward spoke softly again as he

noticed his brother rise from his chair. Although he had consumed as much as everyone else, the king's capacity was legendary, put down by most to the size of his frame, and by a few to long practice. Either way, his head was still clear. 'Please, sit a moment longer.'

Richard sat without hesitation, though he was unsure what his brother might want with him.

'There is something that I need to tell you,' Edward said slowly.

'Sire?' Richard held the king's powerful gaze without flinching.

'Amongst the slain today was the Earl of Warwick.' Edward spoke deliberately, waiting for a reaction.

'Then the largest thorn is removed from your side, Your Grace.' Richard did not hesitate or blink.

'Richard, I know you were close. I would not blame you …'

'Sire,' Richard interrupted. *Too defensive?* he instantly wondered. He continued, though, without missing a beat. 'Warwick was like a father to me. This much is no secret. Much of what I am today I owe to him.'

Richard now felt Edward's gaze weighing more heavily upon him. Searching. Questioning. Silent.

'That,' Richard continued, 'is why his betrayal cut so deeply, as did that of George. Yet in that instant, when he declared against you, he declared against your family. He declared against me, and severed all of those bonds.'

A sudden blaze of anger burned within the young duke's stomach. *What must I do?* he wondered. *How many times must I convince him?*

As quickly as it had come, the blaze was quashed. Richard was well aware that Edward had been betrayed by those he held closest before and needed to remain suspicious. Richard, though, still had an uncomfortable feeling in his gut, as though the embers still smouldered there.

There was a long, heavy silence.

Edward's eyes searched Richard's face for a sign. He wasn't sure what it would be. Shock? Grief? Sadness? Elation? No, not elation. Not even Edward could feel that. Richard had spent the majority of his formative years in Warwick's household, treated as one of his own family. That was the main reason that Edward had been unsure which side Richard would take when things began to go so badly, and why he had been moved when Clarence had joined Warwick. The politician in him remained suspicious, though. Was Richard planted at his side to spy on him? Did he still harbour some loyalty to Edward's most powerful adversary? Edward the brother berated his political caution. Edward the politician challenged his own fraternal desire to trust. Edward the king realized that he must satisfy his political misgivings in order to retain his crown. The question, therefore, had to be asked: How far could he really trust Richard?

'I simply thought that you should hear the news from me.' Edward looked away finally.

The duke felt his lungs re-inflate, only now realizing that he had held his breath throughout the silence without willing it. Despite Edward's apparently genuine concern, Richard knew well that this had been orchestrated to gauge his reaction to the news. The pain returned in the pit of his stomach. His brother still did not trust him. As he rose and left, he refused to betray his sadness at the loss of a man he had thought of as a father. His brother would doubtless have misread this as a form of betrayal. The simple fact was that Richard had loved Warwick and felt every bit as betrayed by him as Edward did. Even that, though, did little to numb the pain of another loss.

'Richard!'

He was snapped from his thoughts by the return of his brother's powerful, regal tone.

He turned slowly. Edward was smiling softly after him.

'We ride tomorrow to pursue the rest of the Lancastrian rebels.'

'Lancastrian rebels?' Richard mused. 'No doubt they refer to us as the Yorkist rebels. Perspective is a powerful and distorting looking glass.'

'When we meet them next, you shall lead out my forces, Richard.' Edward spoke with the solid authority of a monarch bestowing a great honour. And a great honour it was indeed, Richard knew, but a continuation of the endless testing too.

'Thank you, sire,' he conceded graciously, bowing as he stepped back from the tent doorway and took a long slow lungful of the crisp spring air.

Whatever else he felt, he was glad to be home again.

About the author

Matthew Lewis was born and grew up in the West Midlands, and, having obtained a law degree, he currently lives in the beautiful Shropshire countryside with his wife and children. Writing and history, in particular the Wars of the Roses period, have always been his passions, and his novels, *Loyalty* and *Honour*, were born of their joining.

More recently, Matthew has launched a career writing non-fiction, particularly an acclaimed biography of King Richard, *Richard III: Loyalty Binds Me*, and *The Survival of the Princes in the Tower*, which seeks to provide a rounded and complete assessment of the most fascinating mystery in history.

Amazon:	https://www.amazon.co.uk/Matthew-Lewis/e/B0088LP1H0/
Facebook:	https://www.facebook.com/MattLewisAuthor/
Twitter:	https://twitter.com/MattLewisAuthor

Easter 1483

Alex Marchant

An excerpt from *The Order of the White Boar*

The leaf buds were fattening on the trees and the first lambs appearing before Duke Richard returned to Middleham from Pontefract.

He brought with him special sweetmeats from the local bakers to help us break our Lenten fast, after weeks of eating little more than fish from the river and castle ponds. Then, after the solemn Good Friday unveiling of the Cross and the Easter vigil, we pages begged eggs from the kitchens' stockpiles, stored since Ash Wednesday. We boiled them hard in onion-skin dyes to roll them down the slopes in the Duchess's pleasure gardens.

The squires looked on, with good humour or disdain, too old now for such childish pastimes. But, to my surprise, and to the laughter of the ladies who gathered to watch us, not only Masters Lovell, Ratcliffe and Kendall, and various other gentlemen, but Duke Richard himself joined us.

Each of the gentlemen had brought his own egg, except it seemed the Duke.

For a moment, there was disappointment on his face. Lord Lovell declared, 'Then this year I have a chance of winning.'

But the Duke called Alys forward from where she was waiting with the other ladies.

Her dimples showing, she stepped up to him, bringing from behind her back a small casket. As she lifted the lid, there, nestled in black velvet, was the largest egg I had ever seen. It was intricately painted with swirls of red, blue, green, gold, putting our home-dyed hens' eggs to shame.

'The swans of Pontefract obliged me,' said the Duke, picking it up with a flourish.

He beckoned to his son, who had been fidgeting next to me as the scene played out and now leapt forward with sparkling eyes.

'Come, Ed – help me. It is such a fine egg – we shall roll it together.'

So the Duke and his son swept all before them, not only racing the smaller eggs to the bottom of the slope, but surviving without so much as a hair's crack.

Myth and Man

Narrelle M. Harris

Richard endured the whispers as long as he could, and then he went riding. It was that or thrash someone, and since he could not thrash the authors of the insults he heard in his brother's house, riding it would have to be.

Who'd have thought the Duke of Clarence would have so ill-formed a brother?

As though the twist in his spine made him somehow deaf, and the useless arm made him somehow too stupid to notice when people were talking about him.

Young Richard's countenance affrights the milk to curdling.

Richard had been born with his spine out of true and his right arm atrophied, and he had heard such whispers all his life. Sometimes the muscles ached and spasmed awfully, and as a babe and child he had been fractious and difficult to please, he knew. Further, he had not been born under a smiling star, being given rather more to serious thought and plain speaking, which was less pleasing to the ear than flattery.

Perhaps, Richard thought as he kicked the mare to a gallop across the fields towards the woods, if he had known better how to flatter and craft sweet lies, there would have been more kindness. He did not think himself unkind, either, though he was oft accused of the vice. When he had no good thing to say, he kept his counsel, but then he was labelled surly or, worse, *thick-witted*. As though his silence without heralded a silence within.

Insensible dolts. All those braying asses made so much noise it would deafen the birds, and barely a thought made even a timorous noise in those empty heads.

No, Richard thought, I could not and never will be one of those smiling types of cripple, who praise God for their deformities with cherubic countenance, singing foolish songs and playing the jester so that others of better form and weaker brain could smile and laugh, and praise God for their deliverance from affliction. He was a man who spoke plain, and dissembled not, even when it were politic to do so. His words were as straight as his back was bent, and there was no reward for that.

Thou twist-backed lumpen toad.

Richard scowled as he rode through the woods, down the well-trod path. He was not so bad as all that, he believed. He was short, but he walked straight enough, and though his right arm hung stiff and useless, his left was strong and wielded both pen and sword with skill. The limp which plagued him in weariness was hardly noticeable most of the time, and never at all on horseback, where he excelled.

Were I but mounted from daybreak to star-rise, they would never know, he thought bitterly. *I could rule a kingdom from a horse and be counted a great man.*

And yet he was Richard the cripple, Richard the blockhead, Sour-faced Dick and the ape-backed uncle. There were those who thought that his body was a reflection of a soul likewise afflicted. Even his mother thought so. She did not say as much, but she did not deny it either. She loathed to touch him. His brothers teased him, as brothers are wont to do, but they gave more affection to their hunting dogs than they had for him.

How does his mother bear the shame of having birthed him? Wonder not that she prays each day for his soul, and her own.

Well, damn them all to hell, anyway.

Richard reined in the mare to a walk and guided her off the path. He tucked his head to spare his eyes from the whip of low-hanging branches and urged his mount along to the little glade by the brook. None but he visited it. It was a sanctuary, of sorts.

Or, it had been.

As Richard dismounted and led the mare to the water, he knew that someone else was there – a watchful presence in the cool green shadows, the quality of their silence somehow evident above plash and gurgle of the brook over the rocks.

He feigned ignorance of the intruder and spoke softly to the mare, concealing the more covert action of unsheathing his dagger.

A man in gore-streaked armour stumbled from the shadows, sword in hand. His dark blond hair was matted with sweat and blood.

'I would not draw my weapon, if I were you.' The man raised his weapon as though it cost him great effort, but would regardless fight until he fell.

The voice startled Richard with a strange familiarity, as though it were that of a long dead friend. Richard knew of no such friend, however.

The mare at his back, he turned to face the soldier, dagger raised.

'And I would flee, if I were thee. Therefore I must conclude we are not wise men.'

The two men faced each other across the soft grass of the glade, each resolved, fierce, unafraid. The light of startled recognition in their blue eyes likewise the same.

Richard marvelled at this stranger that was no stranger. The armoured man seemed not much older than Richard, though his dark blond hair was longer and greyer than Richard's. His eyes were as lined with suffering as his own. His unshaven cheek and jaw were like Richard's; his nose, his mouth, his ears. It was like seeing into a subtly altered glass.

Even as they stared at one another, the intruder altered. One moment he stood in gory plate and chainmail, then, as suddenly, the man stood naked, scored with wounds that scarcely bled. He fell to his knees, pale as death.

Richard could see plain that though his shoulders

were uneven, this man had two strong arms and two strong legs; that he lacked the painful hunch that drew such callous mirth from Richard's brothers.

In the very next moment, the man's nakedness was covered in a tunic and trews, though head and feet remained bare. He raised his head, defiance and a terrible knowledge in his gaze.

'Oh,' he breathed. 'I am done in.' Grief darkened his gaze, which turned to relief and then, as he looked upon Richard again, to a grim understanding. 'I know you.'

Richard's stout heart beat hard, for he knew witchcraft when he saw it. Yet this better-formed changeling seemed not malicious. A sorrowful light of kindness was in his eyes.

'Greetings, spirit,' said the stranger-like-Richard.

'I am no spirit,' said Richard, defiance defeating any qualm. 'I am Richard, Duke of Gloucester and brother to the Duke of Clarence, on whose lands you trespass.'

'The Duke of Gloucester, you say?'

'Aye. Now name thyself, and what manner of creature you are.'

'I am but a man, Richard, duke and brother of a duke. Those close to me call me Dickon.'

Richard lowered his dagger, wary yet. No one in his life had ever been fond enough to call him his name's dear diminutive.

'If you are a man, Dickon, you are an uncanny one. You bear something of my likeness. Have you been sent to curse me? For I tell you, I am well cursed already.'

'I think … the opposite may be true.' Dickon smiled compassion at him.

It inspired fury in Richard.

'Have you dared come to pity me? I will not take it from you. Let me be plain. I distrust and mislike you. Who sent you to thus insult me with your *pity*?'

Dickon sighed, patient and sad, as yet unpricked by Richard's bristling jabs.

'Perhaps Fate has sent me here, or an angel with some dark humour. Perhaps it was the will of the turning stars, which I saw when I so ignobly died.'

Richard stepped back from this not-quite-mirror. 'I am dead, then.'

'One of us, certainly, and both in time. You do know who I am, then.' Dickon raised a solemn smile.

'I am I,' said Richard carefully, 'Though you are better made. Are you my mother's wish made whole?'

'I have my imperfections,' said Dickon. 'They are but the seeds of yours.'

'But say again. Am I dead?'

'I am not you, although our fates are intertwined,' said Dickon, 'for I too am Richard, once Duke of Gloucester, once King of England, for all too brief a time.'

'King?' breathed Richard. 'Truly, am I?'

'Truly, I was, at great cost.'

'And thou art dead.'

'Me, my wife, my son, my line, my hopes, all lost. Tudors rule England now.'

'And who am I in this host of the lost?'

Dickon shrugged. 'My knowledge comes from somewhere outside me, yet it tells me you are a dream of me.'

Richard was not impressed.

'No dream was ever taunted as I am. No dream has daily curses such as I bear. No dream longs more for recompense. No, Dickon. I believe that you are a dream of *me*.'

Dickon laughed. 'It may be so, but whichever of us is the dreamer or the dreamed, here we are, face to face at the whim of fate.'

Dread filled Richard from toe to top. He, who had always held so strong a sense of self, felt the world shifting under his feet. This Dickon was an apparition, appearing first as warrior, then as corpse, and now as a humble man of no great rank. Why then did Richard feel as though he, himself, was insubstantial, the outline of a man waiting to become real?

In that fearful moment, Richard understood all, because the same terrible knowledge that had come to Dickon now came, full-formed, to his own mind.

Dickon's hand upon his withered arm startled him.

'Be not bitter, Richard.' Dickon's touch was gentle and unflinching.

'Why should I not?' snarled Richard, for he knew now who was real. 'I am but a cracked reflection – a monster made in your likeness. You were not born half made. Your brothers were not cruel to you. Your mother loved you.'

'I'm dead all the same,' said Dickon, rueful-kind. 'Butchered on a battlefield, brutalized and scorned. The victors write my story, and you are he.'

'It is not a good story,' said Richard. 'I wanted to be a good man, but that is not my fate.'

'No.'

For the first time since his lonely childhood, Richard's heart overwhelmed him. His eyes glistened with tears, and his grief made him angry.

'You have come to my only sanctuary to mock me,' he accused. 'Raise up your sword.'

'I will not fight you, Richard.'

'I would rather be cut than mocked to death.'

'I neither mock nor pity you. In your heart is the seed of me. In mine, is a seed of you.'

Richard was not pacified.

'I have a scholar's mind and a fishwife's wit, the humour of a cat and the heart of a lion, and were I but made as straight-limbed as my father, I would be a prince instead of a half-blasted ape. But I can fight, and I will make thee eat thy mocking.'

'I don't want to fight you.'

'Alas for all your wants, as I cry alas for mine.' Richard raised his dagger and poised for combat. 'I have heard counterfeit apologies by the cartload, tendered by those who should love me better by ties of blood. What can you bend to my ear that will make a more pleasing sound than scorn? You cannot hide it from me. Scorn is the music played me from my birth and for all my seven and twenty years, and I will cut the harp strings of your throat if you offer it me.'

Dickon spread his arms, hands palm-up, and head high he stepped up into the point of Richard's blade.

Richard pressed until he knew the dagger must prick Dickon's skin. Dickon betrayed nothing but compassion in his blue eyes.

Richard's knife fell.

'You bewitch me.'

Dickon laid a hand over Richard's heart.

'Storytellers will twist our lives for their own purpose, for their own times. But I know who you are. You are the lie they make of me. We are cuttings from the same root, and though we grow in different ways, we are brothers.'

'I am destined to do terrible things,' said Richard darkly and filled with despair.

'You do not choose your course,' said Dickon, hand still on Richard's heart as though it were a worthy thing. 'Your blood is but the ink with which men write our story.'

Richard's voice was thick with sorrow. 'I wished to be a good man, Dickon, despite all. But I am what the storytellers have made of *you*. No one will ever know me or the man I could have been.'

'*I* know,' said Dickon.

'I will do such wicked, unforgiveable things. I will slaughter what you love and what you hate with equal rancour, to spite a world that cannot love me.' Tears coursed freely down his rough cheeks, grief for everything he would not have and would become. 'None will forgive what I shall become.'

'I forgive you,' said Dickon, and he took Richard, his other self, in his arms. Richard folded into the only tender touch he would ever remember.

On soft green grass, by the singing brook, the king that was and the king to be embraced and wept.

Face pressed to Dickon's shoulder, Richard closed his eyes and bid goodbye to all the choices he might have made. In return came a clear, proud knowledge.

'Your story will live again,' he said quietly to Dickon. 'Your roots in the earth will see the sun once more, and the flower of your truth will bloom. Justice will rise. You will regain the name of champion.'

'I am truly but a man, and flawed withal.'

'And I am but a villain, hand-made for the purpose.' Richard stood tall as his bent back allowed and withdrew from Dickon's embrace. He limped a circle around his other self, and when the turn was done, Richard wore a sly scowl.

'Thus I embrace my storied fate. I will learn to dissemble. I will smile and murder while I smile. I will be the dagger and cut at everything for spite. I will be the twisted soul they say I am, yet so much blacker than their poor imaginations can conjure. I will build a monument of rage and blood and show them: you cannot treat child and man as a beast, but that the beast shall rise and devour them. They are so riven with their petty quarrels and hatreds that I, who hate them all equally, shall conquer. I am a villain and repent not.'

'Of course you must say so,' said Dickon, though for the first time he was troubled. 'So we have been written.'

'None do love me,' said Richard, the grief flaring briefly below the rage.

'I do,' said Dickon, 'for you were made from me.'

'The world will know your truth,' Richard promised him.

'And it will learn from yours,' promised Dickon in return.

Richard was not sure he cared to be a lesson for others, but did not see he had any power in the matter.

'The day grows dark,' said Dickon, although the sun still hung high in the sky. Dickon himself grew faint. Richard could see the brook and the willow through the dead king's translucent chest.

'Brother, don't go,' said Richard, suddenly afraid. *Don't leave me to my fate.*

But Dickon had vanished.

'I am I,' said Richard again to himself. With Dickon gone, he began to feel real again. But then, he thought, truths became myth in time, and in time oft-told stories become truth.

One new truth, however, remained lodged in his heart. A bitter, sacred duty.

None would recall you, brother, the king of but three years' reign. But I will make nations know the name of Richard, Duke of Gloucester; Richard, King of England, third by that name. All shall revile the butcher-king, so that when your day comes again, they will care to learn your history's truth.

It was time to return to his brother's hall, there to follow the unbending path to his future.

'I gird my soul in spite and hate,' he said aloud to the empty glade, 'to play in full my scripted fate.'

Thus resigned, thus embracing, Richard called his mare to him.

Civil war was coming. As he rode towards it, words came to him, a gift from ink and darkness.

I have no brother, I am like no brother;
And this word 'love', which greybeards call divine,
Be resident in men like one another
And not in me: I am myself alone.

Kindred Spirits: Return of the King

Jennifer C. Wilson

As the doors of Leicester Cathedral closed for the final time that day, the ghost of Elizabeth Simpson sank into a chair in the south aisle.

'One of our busiest Saturdays for a while, I think,' she said, not entirely sure who was about, but certain that somebody would be, whether she could see them or not. That was the thing with ghostly communities – transient groups in every way.

'I counted almost five hundred I'm sure, from the ticks in the staff notebook.' The deep, steady voice of her husband Samuel made Elizabeth jump.

'I wish you wouldn't do that,' she scolded. 'Over two hundred years of this, and you still insist on making me jump.'

'Well, you shouldn't spend so long lost in your own thoughts,' her husband retorted. 'Anyway, we must keep our disagreements to ourselves; you never know who is around these days.'

It was true. The cathedral had seen a resurgence in ghostly activity since the reinterment of Richard III in March 2015. Ghosts who had been thought long gone appeared at the nightly gatherings, out of the blue. Between these newer re-arrivals, and the increased visitor numbers amongst the living, some of the longer-term residents were unimpressed.

'Watch out, my dear, Whatton's on his way,' Samuel said, nudging his wife. Elizabeth nodded at the approaching man, but didn't rise. She knew he hated that.

'Simpson,' John Whatton said in greeting as he drew level with them. 'My lady,' he nodded stiffly to Elizabeth. 'More Richard III fans crowding the place out today I see. Honestly, you'd think the novelty would have worn off by now.'

'Don't start all this again, Whatton,' Samuel sighed. 'Westley will be along at any moment, and between the pair of you, it's enough to drive any man back to his tomb.'

'Or woman,' Elizabeth added. Personally, she enjoyed the increase in activity. There were so many interesting people buried in the cathedral after all, and a good number had stayed around, as it were. She glanced across the space, wondering if, and hoping that, Marie Bond would make an appearance that evening. At ninety-seven years old, Marie was the eldest regular resident of the cathedral, and the tales she could tell kept them all entertained – when she was in the mood.

To Elizabeth's delight, the elderly lady appeared, escorted as usual on the willing arm of young Susanna Peppin.

'Marie! So lovely to see you!' Elizabeth rose and greeted her friend and her companion, receiving a tut of derision from Whatton. She ignored him, showing Marie to a chair and ensuring the lady was comfortably settled. They had never managed to secure a permanent solution to the walking-stick problem for her, so human (or spectral) assistance was the best they could offer. Susanna never seemed to mind.

'Somebody thought they saw Richard's ghost outside in the square this afternoon. You haven't heard anything have you?' Marie asked of the group.

'Richard?' John Westley had arrived.

'Yes, Richard. The Third, obviously. Well? Anyone else see anything?'

Elizabeth shook her head. 'I've been out and about most of the day, albeit invisible. I would have seen him if he had come inside.'

'Typical,' scoffed Whatton. 'We are the ones who have stayed here, all these years. He visits – what? – once, since the funeral? And yet it's his ghost they all claim to see. We don't interfere with him and his friends at the Tower; how dare he disturb our days here?'

'But he doesn't, my dear man, I think that's rather the point,' said Marie, rolling her eyes at Elizabeth.

'I just think it's a bit too much. He's nothing but a late-comer. He's been a resident for – what? – a matter of years? And yet he gets all the attention.' John Whatton wasn't finished.

'Well, is it truly any wonder?' Marie snapped at him. 'Apart from a few history students or distant relatives, what exactly do the rest of us have to offer? We should be grateful to have even the bones of a king amongst us, keeping things lively.'

'Hear, hear,' seconded Elizabeth.

'Everyone, everyone!' John Herrick broke into the group's conversation.

'What is it, husband, why the commotion?' Marie demanded.

'He's here, it's true!'

'What?' the spirits demanded in unison.

'Richard. King Richard. With Queen Anne. He's come to visit …'

*

'If we do this, we do it entirely out of sight,' said Queen Anne Neville, looking her husband directly in the eye. Second husband, if anyone wanted to be pedantic, but she didn't. She didn't like to think of her first husband, or marriage, eternally glad the man's ghost had never chosen to try and visit her.

Richard turned to look up at the tower of Leicester Cathedral behind them.

'But I'm sure we were seen, so we might as well just carry on, surely? And so what if a few of my loyal fans spy me here or there?'

'Being seen for a moment by a cathedral resident is one thing, and harmless enough, but I don't want you causing any disruptions. I agreed to come with you if you swore there'd be no trouble. The first hint of it, and I'll be back on the next train out of here, back to London. Without you.'

Anne smiled to herself as she saw Richard's shoulders drop. Whatever the reputation he had at the Tower, even after only a few visits to Westminster Abbey, she knew he was still the charming, gallant knight he had once been, and still a man of his word as a result. Battles and conspiracies hadn't completely erased that.

'Come on, don't you want to get going?'

Richard shook his head. 'Not this evening. There's a fair amount to get through, and I don't want to rush.' He paused. 'I am glad you agreed to come with me. I've only been back briefly, wanted to see what the whole place was like now, a few years down the line.'

'Don't get all soppy on me, Richard Plantagenet. I'm sure there are others who would have visited with you if you had asked. So, if we're not starting now, what's the plan?'

'Well, according to the map,' Richard consulted the pamphlet he'd managed to smuggle out of the visitor centre dedicated to him, disguised in a gust of wind as the automatic doors blew open earlier, 'the tour should actually start at the Blue Boar Inn, so I thought we'd go there this evening, stay over, get a feel for the place, and make a start bright and early tomorrow morning.'

'Is that even possible? Staying over I mean?' Anne raised an eyebrow.

'It's still a hotel. Well, I mean, there's still a hotel on the site. Not the same one, of course. There's bound to be an empty room. Then, tomorrow, we start at Bow Bridge. Again, not original, but still ...'

Anne tilted her head to one side, not immediately convinced by Richard's plan, but it was getting late, and even being able to pass through walls didn't make getting lost in a comparatively strange town an appealing option.

'Very well. Come on, let's see what we can find.'

*

The next morning, having spent a comfortable night in the modern hotel – in between playing with the television and some gentle haunting of a few groups of drunks – Richard and Anne left via the glass automatic doors, leaving behind them the smell of cooking breakfast and light gossip. Consulting the map once again, the couple made their way through the square and across the traffic to the current Bow Bridge, a more modern replacement of the one Richard had crossed that fateful day. Both fateful days, come to think of it.

'Honestly, that woman and her spurs story,' he tutted. 'Things hit bridges, it means nothing. And my head did not hit the parapet on the way back.'

Anne rolled her eyes. She'd worried this would happen. Everything was obviously going to be different, and plenty would most likely be wrong in her husband's eyes. Finding the old Leicester Castle, the next location on their journey, converted into a business school, part of the university, sent him off into another rant as he strode around the series of modern rooms, pointing out what should have been where. Eventually, she managed to usher him into the calm of the church of St Mary de Castro.

'This is better,' said Richard, visibly relaxing.

The place was almost empty, their tour having reached the church before it was open to the public. Only a handful of volunteers were pottering about, getting the place open and ready for the day's visitors. The scent of incense hung heavy in the air, as Richard strolled across to a pile of leaflets and started flicking through.

'At least they have it mostly right,' he said. 'I did

like this place, enjoyed worshipping here when I visited. And look, they've even noted it: *The last monarch to worship here.*' He'd found the portrait of himself hanging on the wall. With a scowl, he noticed the portrait hanging next to it: Henry VI. 'Just a shame there's such a strong Lancastrian presence.'

Richard felt Anne approaching from behind, and knew it was pointless to think too negatively about how things were. Truth was, they were following his Walking Trail, not Henry VI's or Henry Tudor's, around places labelled with their links to him, and nobody else. That wouldn't be the case if nobody cared. And here he was, on a progress of sorts, Anne by his side, having agreed to join him for whatever reason he hadn't fully fathomed yet. After so long, he wouldn't have blamed her for turning him down, but what they'd had was slowly starting to return. He was courting his own wife, and both parties seemed to be enjoying it. Except, she was currently looking at a portrait of her former father-in-law. This would not do.

He coughed quietly, hoping to attract her attention, and help her note that he wasn't pleased with the attention she was paying Henry VI's portrait. As she turned, and made her way towards him, he quickly turned away, not wanting her to see he was troubled by her attention to Lancastrian portraits.

He felt her arm on his, and smiled.

'Shall we rest a while?'

They strolled through to the front of the church, and sat down, tucked out of the way in case visitors suddenly arrived. After an hour of sitting and enjoying the peace, watching the odd tourist make their way around the building, Richard was ready to move on. With a final glance, they passed back through the walls into Castle Yard, and turned towards the Turret Gateway. Here as well, he felt on solid ground. The area, although obviously modern in context, at least had a similar layout to that which he had remembered. The gateway was more crumbled, but he felt he knew where he was.

Reaching the main street, Richard paused for a moment, before pulling himself up straight and looking at the building opposite, another part of the university from what he could see.

'Of course, the Church of the Annunciation is long gone, but apparently some of the original arches are still in the basement.' Even he could hear the forced steadiness in his voice.

Without another word, he slipped through the walls, as Anne followed rapidly behind, only to pass straight through him as he froze just inches from the other side. He was staring into space, not focusing on his surroundings, not focusing on anything. Just blank.

'I can't. I thought I could, thought I could make light of it, but I can't,' he said, his voice starting to crack. He shook his head, trying to rid himself of the image: his own corpse, lying on public display, the wounds of battle there for all to see. His humiliation.

Anne didn't reply, but wrapped him in her arms and pulled him close.

'It's OK,' she said, after a long silence.

Richard nodded into her shoulder. He didn't want to move, but knew he couldn't stay in that building any longer.

'To the next gateway?' he mumbled.

Anne nodded, and pushed him gently away. 'This is why invisible is better,' she said, barely above a whisper.

'Right then.' He turned and led the way back to the street. 'A quick turn around the Newarke Gateway, then on to the main event, as it were?'

*

As they approached the area of the visitor centre, cathedral and Guildhall, Richard felt a weight pressing where his heart would have been. It hadn't been there at the start of the day, or when he'd visited briefly in the past, but today, having seen the rest of the tour, with all those memories flooding back, he was more involved somehow.

'Come on,' encouraged Anne, reaching for his hand. 'It'll be fine. And maybe a touch of gentle haunting wouldn't hurt.'

Richard grinned. He knew he would get his way in the end. He always did. Even if 'the end' involved lying in a lost grave for a couple of centuries, then having the indignity of his feet being cut off by a wall and a carpark built over his head. Yes, he could play the long game. Battles and wars and all that.

The bells started to chime a call to service, as people began to mill about, catching up with each other in twos and threes. He stayed out of sight of the living. These weren't the right targets for a haunting. He would wait and find some suitable tourists later. He offered the crook of his elbow to Anne.

'Shall we attend the service?' he asked.

She replied by slipping her arm through his, and they flickered through the stone wall. To their surprise, a group of ghosts were waiting for them as they entered. The royal couple nodded their greeting, unsure initially what sort of response they would receive.

'Elizabeth and Samuel Simpson, Your Graces.' A man spoke first, stepping forward, his wife alongside him in greeting. Others behind them nodded, a hint of nervousness about their reactions.

'Come to interfere, have you?' John Whatton butted into proceedings.

'No, why would you say that?' said Anne, hurriedly, before Richard could say a word.

Whatton didn't even bother to reply, instead walking off, deliberately turning his back on the Plantagenet pair.

'Well, what a reaction,' she continued, looking to the Simpsons.

They shook their heads, almost in unison.

'Ignore him, Your Grace. Ignore all of us. Please, make yourselves at home, and do enjoy your visit. But do feel free to join us again later, should you wish.'

The small welcome party vanished, each disappearing in their own direction.

'An interesting welcome,' mused Richard, looking around the building properly, wondering who else might be around, and who they might encounter. 'Come on, let's get started. I won't visit the tomb during the service; that doesn't feel right,' he said, as they perched on seats at the back, being careful not to disturb anything as they did so.

For the duration, the pair sat calmly. It wasn't their religion, but both enjoyed the peace that was so often lacking in their daily activities. As the final hymn drew to a close, Anne placed her hand over her husband's. He turned his over and squeezed hers in return. Yes, the day was going well.

The congregation began to disperse, the steady flow outward being gradually replaced by a trickle inward, as visitors realized the service was over, and the cathedral could once again be entered by tourists.

Richard's tomb was at the back, still protected by the strictest security of the velvet rope, in place during the service and not yet removed. People hovered on either side of the space, waiting to go in, whilst Anne and Richard, invisible to all, slipped through.

'It's beautiful,' said Anne, taking Richard's hand again.

'It is,' Richard agreed. 'I mean, yes, it doesn't have the whole effigy thing going on, and some have argued it's a bit plain, but it's certainly striking. Simple and effective I think. A significant improvement on what I had to start with, and a lot more dignified than a carpark space!'

He had listened to and read all the discussion about where his mortal remains should have been located: here in Leicester, in Gloucester, in York, or, where kings had been buried for centuries, in Westminster Abbey.

Standing beside the stone tomb here, at the heart of the cathedral, he was pleased to be in pride of place, his name and motto carved, resplendent and unmissable now.

Finally, the rope was moved aside, and the line of tourists began to snake past, all quiet, respectful and calm. These still weren't the right people, Richard thought. Nor in the right place. He glanced about, and saw his target. A group of schoolchildren, being herded into the main door by a stressed-looking teacher, a few others spread through the group, trying to keep things in order.

'See, I know where I am with a school party,' he said, only half to Anne, as he slipped through the thick walls, across the sanctuary and around to the back of the group. As one of the cathedral volunteers gave an introduction to the site, and told them about Richard's discovery and reburial, he picked his victim, a small, quiet child at back of the group. As the volunteer reached the end of her talk, she smiled at the children and asked if they had any questions.

'Go on, ask if there's a ghost,' Richard whispered.

The small boy he had selected spun around, eyes wide, but he would see nothing.

Richard chuckled to himself, then glanced at Anne to see whether she had decided to join him. She had not, but was smiling at him, gently shaking her head.

He continued around the group. For his next victim, he chose something different. A small girl, loitering at the back of the group, her pigtails were just too much to resist, especially as there was nobody behind her she could blame. After emitting a small squeak, and being subsequently scolded, she hurried to the front of the column, staying as close to her teacher as possible.

After distracting a couple of the volunteers and adults, he returned to Anne, now sitting in St George's chapel, looking up at the carvings and stained glass windows.

'It's good to get it out of your system now and then,' he said, joining her.

'On to the visitor centre, then?' she replied.
Richard nodded. This was going to be interesting.

*

He knew the layout from his previous visit, but that time, he hadn't felt up to going as far as seeing his original grave-site, or what they had done around the place, in terms of exhibition and presentation. This time, with Anne at his side, he knew he had to do it. But he would do it properly, follow the route, see how things had been done, enjoy – if that was the right word – the build-up to the site itself.

Ignoring the doors and crowds waiting patiently to pay their entry fees, Richard and Anne made their way into the exhibition, stopping to watch the video which was just about to restart on a wall-sized screen, behind a mocked-up medieval throne.

'I don't want a running commentary of what you're not happy about, do you understand?' said Anne, instantly distracted by a representation of herself, walking on to the screen and giving her name to the watching group. 'Well – well, I never. That's meant to be me! I didn't think I would feature.'

'Ah, but of course you feature; you should be the star of the show,' teased Richard, nudging her with his shoulder.

She shushed him, and they made their way into the exhibition proper.

*

To Anne's surprise, Richard kept his own counsel throughout most of the exhibition. The history, after all, had been discussed and disputed for years; there was little point a ghost arguing with what was written now – what could he do about it anyway? It was the science that was fascinating. Yes, the story of how the dig had come about, and the physical side of actually finding his skeleton was interesting, but all those analyses? The fact that they could determine (with some accuracy, they both had to confess) what his diet had comprised, how tall he had been, and what sort of world he had inhabited, that was close to witchcraft in Anne's and Richard's eyes.

'All this can be told from our bones,' said Richard, staring at the mock-up of his own skeleton, on display in the centre of the room.

'And that's just for now,' Anne replied, hoping he wouldn't be distracted by the signs about fatal injuries and weapons of the day. 'I mean, we would never have imagined them doing this in our day, but look how much has changed just in the last century.'

Finally, making their way downstairs, they approached the small, chapel-like area that enclosed his original grave, in the now famous carpark.

Richard paused, still uncertain, only to find himself being urged on by Anne.

'You can do this, husband,' she whispered, before smiling encouragement.

'Whether I can or I can't, I have to,' he replied.

They waited at the entrance, waiting for a small group to leave; this was no place for a haunting. Seeing nobody about to follow them, Richard took Anne's hand, and stepped through the doorway.

The calm struck him first. Yes, it looked like a chapel, built over the small site, but somehow it felt like one too. With pale stone walls, low benches and high windows, it felt a positive space. Then he saw the glass. Rising up from the floor, right to the ceiling – the grave was encased entirely.

Slowly, avoiding looking at the guide sitting to one side, Richard stepped forward, steadying himself.

He could do this. Of course he could.

The last time he had looked down on this grave, it had been surrounded by the buildings of Greyfriars, not yet topped with any monument, but covered in, prayers still being said for his soul. He hadn't stayed long after his burial, hadn't seen the point. London was where things were happening, London was where decisions were being made, so London was where he had gone – once he was used to his ghostly form.

The Tower of London had become home so quickly, he'd hardly travelled since, beyond the odd foray; being so far away, and with Anne by his side, he felt a strength he had occasionally found lacking lately.

'It's beautiful.' Anne's voice broke into his train of thought. She moved up to the glass, then half a heartbeat later, jumped back in shock, staring at Richard.

'What is it?' he asked, moving forward to join her. Then he saw it.

A projector, hidden in the top of the glass, created an image within the grave – one that was too perfect a depiction of Richard's skeleton for either of them to be comfortable with it.

'That's how he left you?' asked Anne, in a whisper.

'Yep. But we, well, I, would have done the same. It was never just about the battle, was it? What you did next was always just as important.'

'But – when you compare what we had – in terms of our graves ... I'm sorry.' She reached for his hand.

'It's amended now, that's all that matters. I've got my grave, pride of place, right in the heart of the cathedral, my name and motto given their dues.'

Richard watched the projection fade in and out a few more times before speaking again.

'I'm glad we came back, but I think this is it now. Onwards and upwards.'

'Not your white light? You wouldn't leave us all?' There was the hint of a shake to Anne's voice.

'Leave? Who mentioned leaving? Well, leaving here, yes, but that's it. No, I don't intend to go anywhere anytime soon; things are just starting to get fun, after all. Being here, it was important, but this is the past for me now. They've found me, reburied me, and my reputation is turning around quite nicely.' He put his arm around her shoulders. 'Me and you – how about we head back to London, to our respective homes, but on the way, we make ourselves a plan? Think of all the places we can visit, the fun we can have; it'll be like the last five hundred odd years never even happened. How about it?'

Anne pulled away from Richard, and looked him in the eye.

'Go travelling?'

'A royal progress. I hear the Scots queen went on one. Very successful it was too, by all accounts.'

Anne smiled. 'A royal progress. Yes, I like that idea. All right, I'm in.'

Richard clapped his hands together and grinned.

'An excellent decision, I assure you. So, back to the Tower? It's time we were planning.'

With a final glance at the projected image of his skeleton in his cramped, undignified grave, Richard and Anne made their way out of the exhibition, nodded to two of the cathedral's ghosts, loitering at the great wooden door, and made their way towards the station.

About the author

Jennifer C. Wilson is a marine biologist by training, who developed an equal passion for history whilst stalking Mary, Queen of Scots on childhood holidays (she has since moved on to Richard III). She completed her BSc and MSc at the University of Hull, and has worked as a marine environmental consultant since graduating. Enrolling on an adult education workshop on her return to the north-east of England reignited her pastime of creative writing, and she has been filling notebooks ever since.

In 2014, Jennifer won the Story Tyne short story competition, and has been working on a number of projects since, including co-hosting the North Tyneside Writers' Circle.

Her *Kindred Spirits* novels are published by Crooked Cat Books and her timeslip novella *The Last Plantagenet?* by Ocelot Press.

Website:	https://jennifercwilsonwriter.wordpress.com/
Amazon:	https://www.amazon.co.uk/Jennifer-Wilson/e/B018UBP1ZO/
Facebook:	https://www.facebook.com/jennifercwilsonwriter/
Twitter:	https://twitter.com/inkjunkie1984
Instagram:	https://www.instagram.com/jennifercwilsonwriter/

15

Beyond the Rood

Wendy Johnson

They brought him here as the usurper rode out. Naked, dirty, bloodstained, trussed in a sling formed of a grubby bedsheet. Like a slaughtered beast: while none remained to weep for him, but me.

Enemies everywhere. Soldiers fresh from the field, renegade nobility, those who have betrayed my master and cleave instead to the victor: the unknown. Whether they will use this man as a puppet, or affect some feigned, belated sense of allegiance, they will find no greater king than he who now lies beyond the rood.

A friary church, a hole hastily dug by fearful monks. No hearse, no pall, no requiem; no waxen image offered up, to melt away as his soul flies to God. No tomb chest, no obit, no chantry prayers. No coffin, no shroud, no sweet herbs. A crude grave under the feet of the friars, laudations for the new king echoing above.

Vespers is ended; the last candle snuffed out. Sandaled feet have slapped the night stairs. A residue of prayer hovers like incense.

In the silence there is only my master and me. It is time. I lay down my sword, steel scraping stone, and shrink inside my hood. By the dim, sanguine glow of the sanctuary lamp, I inch forward, towards the quire.

Unaccompanied, unseen. I kneel before the grave.
Fealty. Loyalty. Ricardus Rex.

Call for contributions

Would you like the chance to have a story included in a future anthology of Ricardian tales? Have you already written one, or perhaps have an idea and have yet to put it down on paper (or onscreen)? Is poetry more your thing?

Alex Marchant is planning a further anthology of fiction and perhaps poetry inspired by King Richard III towards the end of 2019. If you would like to have a piece considered for inclusion, please follow and check Alex's blog or Facebook page for announcements over the next few months: https://alexmarchantblog.wordpress.com and https://www.facebook.com/AlexMarchantAuthor/.

Printed in Poland
by Amazon Fulfillment
Poland Sp. z o.o., Wrocław